Love Knows My Name

Aspiring Love Collection - Volume 1

Wanda B. Campbell ~ Linda Leigh Hargrove
Alicia Fleming ~ Yolanda Johnson Bryant
T.A. Beasley ~ Naa Harper ~ Leslie K. Howard
Annie Johnson ~ Tyora Moody

Tymm Publishing LLC
Columbia, SC

Love Knows My Name
Aspiring Love Collection: Volume 1

Paperback ISBN: 978-1-7336967-0-8
Ebook ISBN: 978-1-7336967-1-5

Published by Tymm Publishing LLC
701 Gervais Street, Suite 150-185
Columbia, SC 29201
www.tymmpublishing.com

Cover Design: TywebbinCreations.com
Editing: Felicia Murrell

Dedication

This anthology is dedicated to the woman (or man) who has given up on love. We never know who God may place in our paths. Remain open to the possibilities.

Acknowledgements

This anthology includes stories from both veteran and first-time authors, all passionately sharing their love of romance through their stories. *Love Knows My Name* would not exist without the contributions of the following authors: Wanda B. Campbell, Linda Leigh Hargrove, Alicia Fleming, Yolanda Johnson Bryant, T.A. Beasley, Naa Harper, Leslie K. Howard and Annie Johnson. We want to express a huge thanks to Felicia Murrell for her patient editing of each co-author's short story. We hope each story leaves the reader with a smile.

Table of Contents

Listing of Short Stories

Lasting Impressions **by Wanda B. Campbell**

Working as an ICU nurse offers Kaymar Washington many rewards, but a cure for loneliness isn't one of them. Patient Johnny Twenty-five changes everything. With ease, her new patient fills her hidden desire for companionship and gives her something more than charity work to look forward to. As the attraction between nurse and patient grows, will Kaymar remove the emotional walls so her heart can heal? If only her patient wasn't comatose and knew she exists.

Dancing on the Moon **by Linda Leigh Hargrove**

Dr. Katrina Mason loves teaching college math. It's a rewarding departure from her past vocation as a stripper. When an abusive relationship forces her to take a job at a high school in another state, she's pleasantly surprised how much she enjoys it. That is, until she gets a lewd unsigned note to the school's Valentine dance using her old stage name. When handsome Principal Nate Thomas finds out about her provocative past, will he be inviting her to leave the job? In the end, what Nate teaches Katrina about love will have her feeling like she's dancing on the moon.

Love Called My Name by Alicia Fleming

When you suddenly lose someone you love, you tend to guard your heart more carefully. You tend to be hesitant about letting people get close to you and falling in love again. After all, only the people that are close to you, can hurt you. Sierra Ramsey meets Blaine Johnson

in her grief care support group. As their friendship blossoms, Sierra lets her guard down and learns to love again. But, she's still indecisive about her choice. When love calls your name again, after having your heart broken, will you answer? Find out how Sierra goes from a broken heart to a heart full of unbelievable joy.

For the Love of You by Yolanda Johnson-Bryant

After a failed marriage, Serena Collins was done with relationships, that is until Gerard Nelson. The two fall in love, and Gerard is all that Serena has dreamed of and more. A weekend trip to an exotic location ends abruptly with bad news. After the prognosis of terminal illness, the couple has to decide if a lifetime of love is worth the little time they have. Certain Gerard is her forever soulmate, Serena is content with the life she's lived. That is until Greg Pierce. Is this divine intervention? Or will Serena throw away a second chance at love?"

A Coffee Shop Connection by T.A. Beasley

Renee Spencer is running late for work but knows she'll be no good for anyone without her morning coffee from Rose's Coffee Cafe. When she arrives, the line is so long, forcing her to take a different route into an alternative coffee shop that may provide more than just morning coffee. David Brock is on his way to work when he stops to help a friend. He arrives at his coffee shop to help with the morning rush, and a new customer catches his eye. Unbeknownst to Renee, her detour may be fate trying to brighten up her day.

A Timeless Love by Naa Harper

Candace Parker is a teenage girl with big dreams and a lot to offer. At seventeen, she is smart, beautiful, and ready to take her life to the next level. When she catches the unrelenting eye and attention of Michael Taylor, star quarterback of Olive's high school football team, her world is wrecked and turned upside down. Dreams she once had are now gone. It is not until she makes the decision to leave Farmville, Virginia, that what seemed impossible, becomes a possible reality. When she attends the regularly scheduled game night and dinner at a friend's house, there is one guest she is not expecting.

One Day I'll Be Gone by Leslie K. Howard

Jeanette, a meek young college student gets caught up in a warm, attentive whirlwind named Thomas Watson. But after they marry, everything about Tom changes. Tom has everything: Jeanette, his Christian wife, a good job and a comfortable place to live. For him, life is perfect. In reality, his alcoholism, partying and affairs with other women has his life spiraling out of control. To the world around her Janette looks happy but behind the façade, her life is in ruins. An apocalyptic event rocks Tom's world and he discovers his Jenny is gone. Did Janette's prophetic warning of *One Day I'll Be Gone* come true?

Spring Blues by Annie Johnson

Physical therapist Spring Vaughn is still struggling with a past tumultuous relationship. When DeMarco Blues, a professional football player, becomes her latest patient, she can't deny her attraction. But the last thing she wants is another relationship with an athlete. She surmises DeMarco is like any typical player with a fleet of women at his feet. DeMarco is determined to soften her hard heart and teach Spring to trust in love again. Will Spring realize DeMarco is exactly what she needs before it's too late?

The Replacement Date by Tyora Moody

Five years after a rocky divorce, Donna Madison is out on her first date. But when she is stood up by her date, she's not too upset because a surprise "replacement" date saves the night. The man who shows up at her table is a childhood friend she hadn't seen in fifteen years. Maxwell Anderson is no ordinary blast from the past, and Donna can't help but wonder if the unexpected meeting has divine purposes.

Lasting Impressions
Wanda B. Campbell

Monday 2:41 p.m.

Three years of working at the medical center and Kaymar still had to arrive forty-five minutes early for her scheduled shift just to find a parking space. She circled three levels of the parking garage twice and gritted her teeth. $150 deducted from her paycheck for the privilege of arriving to work frustrated. Why couldn't management assign a parking stall number in exchange for her hefty paycheck deduction? She'd asked that very question at each of the quarterly employee forums hosted by the executive management team without remedy.

The wheels on the SUV to the right hugged the white parking strip of the empty space, but she maneuvered her Honda into the narrow stall with precision. Kaymar sucked in her abdominal muscles and tiptoed between her car and the Ford on the left. She glanced at her watch before retrieving her travel bag from the trunk. Only fifteen minutes remained before the start of her shift in ICU, waiting for the elevator was not an option so she sprinted towards the stairwell. Fifteen minutes and forty-five seconds later, Kaymar was at the nurse's station dressed in gray scrubs receiving a patient's report.

Tonight would be busier than the extra shift she worked last night. In addition to a myocardial infarction patient, a new comatose patient was added to her workload. Kaymar discreetly rolled her eyes at the charge nurse, April. She seemed to always draw the shortest straw. Of the five nurses on the unit, she was the only one with two patients. Did she have a *Please pick me I want to work harder than the other nurses collecting a check* sign on her forehead? When she previously brought the disparity to the charge nurse's attention, April explained that she trusted Kaymar's ability and skill level. Instead of a compliment, Kaymar took the explanation as an excuse for being taken advantage of.

At twenty-eight, Kaymar had endured several relationships where she'd given her heart and soul to someone who reciprocated by shattering her heart and draining her resources. Her nurturing nature made her a magnet for being taken advantaged. A sob story was her kryptonite. One sad story and an invisible "S" appeared across her chest. She'd be off to save those in need, regardless of the cost. The problem was, instead of feeling fulfilled, Kaymar often felt empty and used. After her last breakup, she vowed to direct all of her care and attention towards her patients. They couldn't hurt or take advantage of her, and the ones that recovered were always appreciative of her services. The families of the deceased patients even thanked her for providing comfort to their loved ones and often brought her little gifts.

Maybe April was sincere in her reason for assigning her the heavier load. Kaymar received the most STARS on the unit. STARS were comment cards filled out by staff, patients, and patient families giving accolades to staff for providing good service and care. It was hard for Kaymar to trust people after being hurt so many times. "You can't judge the world by a few bad apples. Your heart is too good for that," her mother reminded her when Kaymar shied away from new people. Her mother was probably right, but Kaymar wasn't willing to risk her heart again.

Kaymar read the notes and orders for Mrs. Fairview, the heart attack patient in Bed B, and decided to check on her before the comatose patient. Mrs. Fairview's heart attack had occurred twenty-eight hours earlier and left her in critical condition. After administering medication, Kaymar checked the feeding tube and the catheter in her leg, measuring the pressure in her chest. She checked her vitals and electronically charted her notes, offering silent words of thanks for Mrs. Fairview's slight improvement from the night before. Kaymar always evoked divine intervention on behalf of her patients. Her Christian faith taught her to believe in miracles, and she had witnessed numerous unexplained recoveries.

"Hey, Kay. It looks like your MI patient is doing better."

Kaymar continued to surf her next patient's electronic chart. She knew the voice belonged to her colleague, Monica. The twenty-something was always perky and talked more than Kaymar cared to listen.

"Yeah, she's progressing well," Kaymar answered without making eye contact, hoping Monica would get a clue and keep it moving.

"She's only fifty-four with a heart attack. You just never know. What hot plans do you have for this weekend? I'm going ziplining with my BFF..."

And just like that, diarrhea of the mouth commenced. "Excuse me, Monica," Kaymar interrupted, "I have to check on my new patient." She gathered her paperwork and made a dash to Bed D before Monica got her second wind.

Kaymar didn't have a real name for the African-American male laying comatose in Bed D with a Glasgow Coma Scale of 11, only an alias. Patient Johnny Twenty-five was brought in as a trauma, the victim of aggravated robbery. From the facial swelling and bruises on his knuckles, Johnny Twenty-five wasn't a passive victim. He must have fought hard until suffering a traumatic brain injury, the result of blunt force by a metal object according to the EMT's report.

Kaymar took longer than normal with her visual examination. The length of his body nearly covered the entire bed, and she guessed his height around six feet or more. His legs were stocky and muscular like his arms. The six-pack and protruding pectorals were clear indicators of his belief in exercise and physical fitness. His swollen lips hung open, resting at a crooked slant. She guessed behind his closed eyelids were dark brown eyes. The shape of his head was boxed at the top and square at the chin. The edges of his short hair looked as if he'd recently had a haircut. Maybe it was her weakness for dark chocolate men, but even with a swollen head, discolored face and feeding tube, Johnny Twenty-five was somewhat handsome.

"Hello, my name is Kaymar." As was her routine with all new patients, Kaymar introduced herself. "I'll be your nurse for the next twelve hours. If the six letters are too much, Kay is fine," she added for humor. Kaymar didn't know if Johnny Twenty-five could hear her or not, but she wanted him to know he would be well cared for in case he could.

She continued reading the monitors and charting the Electronic Medical Records. More than once, Kaymar found her eyes traveling back to Johnny Twenty-five's face as she studied his EMR. Who was this man, and why was he a target of violence? The intake form stated no identifying information, jewelry, or car keys were found at the scene. Was he driving a fancy car at the time of the attack? Did he occupy a legal job or hustle on the side? Was there a Mrs. Johnny Twenty-five wondering why he hadn't come home?

The entire shift, Kaymar alternated her attention and time between her two patients, spending considerably more time with Johnny Twenty-five. She couldn't identify why, but the battered and bruised man intrigued her. Instead of the usual inward meditations, Kaymar prayed audibly for Johnny Twenty-five's recovery before giving report to the next shift nurse. Inside the locker room, Kaymar found herself humming while she exchanged her scrubs for street clothing. The melodic sound ceased once she recognized what she was doing. Humming was reserved for happy times. Happiness hadn't visited Kaymar in a long time.

Tuesday, 8:39 a.m.

Kaymar glanced over at the clock on her nightstand and closed her devotional. She wondered why she wasn't sleepy. Normally, her feet didn't touch the floor before 10:00 a.m., but today was different. She was different, and she didn't know why. She'd been awake, sitting up in bed, for over an hour. With only four hours of sleep, she should have been exhausted. Her usual after work routine of showering and climbing into bed was interrupted by thoughts of Mr. Johnny Twenty-Five. After climbing into bed, Kaymar had surfed the Internet for news coverage on her patient's assault. She'd never done that before, but an unquenchable thirst to learn more about the dark chocolate man in Bed D had outweighed her need for sleep.

All three online sites for Bay area local news had brief coverage of a carjacking and an assault on a commuter train. Each incidence cited an unidentified African American male victim in serious condition at a local hospital – her hospital. Her gut told her the commuter train victim was Johnny Twenty-five. That revelation left her with more questions. "I wonder where he was going?" She whispered the question, and then scolded herself. "Why does it matter, and why should I care? He's just another patient." She shut down the computer and turned off the bedroom lamp, staring into the darkness until she fell asleep.

Her first conscious thoughts of the morning, after the sunrays disturbed her sleep, were of her patient. Instead of turning over and snuggling under the cover, Kaymar stretched and slipped to her knees. She prayed her normal supplications then added both patients to the list. With her prayer and meditation complete before nine, she didn't know what to do with the extra hour. Laundry or clean out the refrigerator? She decided to make breakfast.

Despite opting for sleep five days a week over preparing breakfast, it remained her favorite meal of the day. She still sprayed her waffles and pancakes with whipped cream like her mother used to. Only now, she replaced maple syrup with fresh fruit and substituted uncured turkey bacon for pork. The telephone rung seconds after she cut into the mini stack of pancakes.

"Hey, Ma. What's up?" She greeted the caller without checking the caller ID. Only her mother called her landline.

"Why do you sound so alert this morning?"

Kaymar continued cutting. "Huh? Oh, nothing. It's a beautiful day the Lord has made, and I will rejoice and be glad in it," she sang, then stuck a forkful of pancakes in her mouth.

"I thought you worked last night. I didn't know you had a date." Her mother's voice filled with excitement. "Tell me all about it."

Kaymar rolled her eyes. She hated how her mother always equated happiness with having a man around. "Mother, I did work last night. Very hard, I might add."

"Well, the last time you sounded this cheerful before noon you had a boyfriend. And, stop rolling your eyes. You know the spirit allows me to see through telephone wire and walls."

Kaymar nearly choked laughing at her mother. Her mom was always elevating her mother's intuition to superpower status. "Mama, you've been saying that for years."

"And, I've been right for years." Her mother laughed. "Now what's his name?"

"Seriously, Ma, it's just me and Jesus...and my patients."

"Taking care of other folks won't replace the need you have for someone to love and take care of you."

Kaymar's happy world came crashing down. Her unspoken need for companionship had led her to yield her virginity to her last boyfriend, who forgot to mention he already had a family. She broke her purity vow when he declared his undying love for her and presented her with a ring. Not long after, he asked to borrow money to purchase a car. Kaymar gave him the money as an investment in their future. Blinded by what she thought was love, she believed they would marry. Right up until the moment she ran into him on a chance trip at a Wal-Mart across town. He, along with a woman and two kids, were ahead of her in the checkout line. The kids called him daddy and the woman wore a ring similar to the one Kaymar had on her left ring finger. The moment their eyes met, he looked frightened. But he recovered quickly and continued playing with his kids as if his side chick wasn't standing behind him. He walked out of the store and out of Kaymar's life.

That was two years ago. No matter how much she wanted to love and be loved, she maintained the brick wall around her heart with tenacity.

She shook the memory away. "Ma, I'm not going there."

"Baby, maybe you should, it's been a while."

She pushed her plate away; the pancakes were no longer appetizing. "You're right, Ma. I do need a companion to keep me warm at night. Someone I can trust with my innermost feelings would be nice too."

"That's what I'm talking about, baby. God never intended for us to go through this life alone."

"And it wouldn't hurt if he were dark and handsome, either."

"Lord, let him be fine!"

Kaymar pictured her mother waving her hands in the air, giving praise to God. "Thanks so much, Ma, for reminding me of how lonely I am and giving me the perfect solution. I'm getting a dog."

"You're getting a what?" Her mother's voice dropped two octaves.

"That's right, Ma. Since you insist I have a warm body in my life, I'm getting a dog. A big, black hairy dog." Kaymar laughed.

"That is not what I had in mind, Kaymar Washington." Her mother snarled.

"Of course not, Ma. But, that's my solution for you and everyone else insisting I need someone in my life."

"You know—"

Kaymar cut her off. "Ma, I have to go. Love at the pound awaits me." She disconnected the call before her mother could voice more protests. She pulled the plate back, reveling in besting her mother. Kaymar had no intention of getting a dog anytime soon, but her mother didn't know that.

Tuesday, 3:06 p.m.

During shift report, Kaymar learned Mrs. Fairview had improved enough to transfer to the step-down unit. "Thank, God," she whispered.

"You did a great job taking care of her," April complimented. "Her family asked me to convey their gratitude."

"Thank you," Kaymar responded with humility. "Just doing my job."

"Mr. Turner's family is in the waiting room in case you'd like to meet them."

"Mr. Turner?" Kaymar asked as April turned to leave.

"Did I forget to tell you? Johnny Twenty-five was identified this morning. His name is Jamal Turner. He was assaulted on a commuter train while trying to stop some kids from robbing an elderly woman. You may have heard about it on the news."

"Wow." Kaymar was amazed she'd guessed correctly.

"There hasn't been much change in his condition, but at least he's stable. And now his family is here," April continued. "Maybe that will help him come out of the coma."

"Yeah, the presence of family is always good." Kaymar wondered what his family dynamics were like.

"Have a good shift."

"Thanks, you too." Before April left the nurse's station, Kaymar logged into the EMR to learn more about the patient in Bed D now that he had a name.

Jamal Turner was thirty-one years old. They shared the same birth month. She'd been fairly accurate at guessing his height. Jamal Turner was six-feet two-inches tall. She speculated if he rode the commuter train regularly to work based on his suburban address. The remaining details revealed medical things, his blood type, allergies, but nothing about his marital status.

She shook her head. Why do I care? He's just another patient.

"Hello, Jamal. It's me, Kaymar. I will be your nurse again this evening. I hope you don't mind me addressing you by your first name." She went about her routine of checking and charting his vitals. As if he could hear, she continued to address him, explaining every task as she worked. The swelling in his head and lips had decreased and she told him as much. Talking to comatose patients wasn't new for Kaymar, but the arm and hand massage after checking the Foley catheter was. She also massaged his lower legs and feet, wanting to make sure his extremities received adequate circulation. At least, that's the explanation she fed her psyche.

"It's time for me to meet your family," she said, after a brief audible prayer for his recovery. "I'll be right back, don't move." She laughed at her corny joke but sobered before rounding the corner leading to the ICU waiting room.

She spotted Jamal's father immediately. Even with his eyes closed and salted temples, the resemblance was noticeable. He was holding hands with a lady Kaymar assumed was Jamal's mother and a male and female. Kaymar waited until the gentleman finished praying before approaching the group.

"Hello. Are you the family of the patient in Bed D, Jamal Turner?" She asked for confirmation before disclosing patient information.

"Yes," the gentleman answered for the group. His eyes were filled with worry. "Jamal is our son. These are our other children. Is he awake?"

"Has there been a change? Is my baby awake yet? Please tell me he'll wake up and be his old self." His mother stepped forward but didn't release the father's hand.

Kaymar's heart ached for them. As much as she wanted to ease their worries, she couldn't promise their desired outcome. "My name is Kaymar. I'll be caring for your son on the swing shift during the week as long as he's in ICU." Noticing the family still held hands, she didn't extend hers. "Mr. Turner is not awake, yet. His vitals remain stable, and some of the facial swelling has gone done." She wanted to ease their anxiety. "You may sit with him for a few minutes, but only two at a time."

"I want to go this time," the young woman answered. "I need to see my brother." Her beauty made Kaymar thankful she was his sister and not a girlfriend or wife.

"No, I'm going," the brother argued.

"Your mother and I are going first," the patriarchal head declared.

"Each of you will be able to spend time with him. As long as Mr. Turner's vitals remain stable, you can rotate throughout my shift," she assured them. "In the meantime, is there anything I should know about your son that will assist in his care? Is there anything special I can do to help stimulate him? Some comatose patients can hear. I encourage you to talk or read to him during your visits."

"He likes music," the mother answered in almost a whisper. "The only time he doesn't have headphones on is when he's driving. Then the radio is blasting. He loves that gospel hip-hop stuff. Oh, God," her voice broke, "he's got to wake up."

"Thanks for sharing that. I can't guarantee your son's outcome, but I promise to administer my best care. I noticed Christianity is noted as religious preference."

Mr. Turner nodded. "He was reared in church, teaches the youth now.

"I'll also say a prayer for him."

"Thank you," Mrs. Turner said.

Kaymar took a step backward. "I need to get back to my patient. I will come and get you soon."

Kaymar trekked back to the nurse's station, acknowledging how blessed Jamal Turner was. He was loved and cherished by his family and had what appeared to be a solid foundation, his faith. And he was cute. "Oh, God," she pleaded as his mother had, "he has to wake up."

Friday, 6:10 p.m.

"You really enjoy your work, don't you?" Mrs. Turner said from behind.

The lyrics to Kaymar's favorite worship song hung in her throat as she turned around. She thought she and Jamal were alone. Singing to Jamal had become routine. "Huh?"

"You're the most devoted nurse I have ever seen." Her gratitude did nothing to conceal her worry.

Kaymar stood to allow Mrs. Turner access to Jamal's bedside.

"I've been watching you these past three days. You spend most of your shift at my son's bedside." The back of Mrs. Turner's hand stroked Jamal's right cheek. "The swelling is almost gone. Is all of this part of your job?"

Kaymar cleared her throat to steady her voice. Mrs. Turner made her nervous. "All of what, ma'am?"

"The reading. The singing. The talking. Everything. The entire family has noticed. You treat my son as if he's wide awake – like you guys are old friends." She cupped his cheeks. "He's losing weight. Yesterday, I overheard you telling him what you had for dinner and sharing your favorite movies." Her hands moved to his head

13

where the bandage covering the open wound lay. "I hope his hair grows back. He's not vain, but I don't think he would like a bald spot in the middle of his head. Turning to Kaymar, she asked, "So, do you spend this much time with all of your patients?"

The temperature in ICU was set to cool but sweat moistened Kaymar's hands. Not only did Mrs. Turner make her nervous, Kaymar didn't like the honest answer to her question. True, she was an excellent nurse, but even Kaymar had to admit the quality and quantity of time she spent with Jamal was beyond the normal nurse-patient scope. Since the ICU census was low, Jamal Turner had been her sole patient for three days. She'd taken advantage, spending as much time as possible with him —reading everything from scripture to online news and magazines from the waiting room and singing. Singing was something she hadn't done since quitting the choir after her last breakup, too ashamed to sing in God's house. She also talked a lot about her personal life to Jamal. Why she didn't know, but if Jamal was coherent, he would know her favorite color, movie, car, food, dream vacation and perfume. Had her life become so boring and mundane? She'd found companionship in someone who may not even know she was alive. She didn't view her time with Jamal as a chore. For two days she had prayed the ICU census would remain low, allowing her more time with him. Kaymar enjoyed taking care of Jamal, but now as Mrs. Turner pressed for an answer, Kaymar considered her actions may not have been the wisest thing to do.

"Well, Mrs. Turner," she stuttered.

"Please, Olivia is fine. After all you've done for my son, I think it's appropriate."

Kaymar swallowed hard. "Okay, Olivia. I try to give all of my patients the highest level of care. Jamal is such an easy person to care for." She hoped Olivia would accept her answer. She couldn't even admit to her own mother how unfulfilled her life was. *I really do need a dog.*

Olivia shrugged. "Well, if you say so. You spend more time with him than his wife did."

Kaymar's heart dropped to her stomach. Wife? No one had mentioned a wife. Where was she? "I didn't realize Jamal is married."

"He's not anymore, thank God. That woman was no good for him, but he was too in love to believe otherwise." Olivia formed quotation marks in the air with her fingers around the word love. "Instead of a husband, she saw him as a financier for her shopping sprees and trips with her girlfriends. And, let's not forget the luxury car she just had to have. The girl didn't even work or go to school. Didn't do nothing. Just hung out all day with God knows who. She didn't know how to cook or do laundry. Jamal almost killed himself working two full-time jobs to keep up with her bills." She stepped away from her son, closer to Kaymar and whispered, "I was so glad when she ran off with that musician and divorced him. Otherwise, Jamal would have killed himself trying to honor his vows. Even after he found out she was cheating, he still tried to make it work. He's just now recovering from the financial mountain she left." Olivia paused and turned back toward Jamal. "My son deserves so much more than this. Oh God, he just has to pull through."

Olivia's voice cracked, and Kaymar left her alone with her son. She didn't want to see her cry, and Kaymar needed to gather her own emotions. Why had her heart nearly stopped when a wife was mentioned? And why did her heart ache at the betrayal Jamal endured? There was so much she didn't understand, but Kaymar had to admit, the more she learned about Jamal Turner, the more she liked. The fact that he lay in a coma was proof he placed others before himself. His willingness to forgive his unfaithful wife demonstrated he valued commitment. Jamal Turner validated her mother's belief that good men still existed. "That's something else we have in common. We're both horrible at selecting companions," she mumbled. That would change today. Kaymar would begin her search for a dog before the night was over.

Tonight, the time she spent with Jamal at the end of her shift before giving report to the night-shift nurse was different. It was Friday, and unless she was called in for an extra shift, Kaymar wouldn't see Jamal for two days. She couldn't recall a previous time when leaving a patient for the weekend saddened her, but the thought of not seeing Jamal did just that. Medically, if his Glasgow continued to improve, Jamal would be leaving the ICU soon. As much as she wanted him to recover, Kaymar wasn't prepared for that either.

"I'm going to miss you, Jamal. Especially our talks," she mused and stroked his cheek. "You don't look half bad. I bet you clean up good. There's a chance you won't be here when I return. Hopefully, you'll have a new home in the step-down unit." She squeezed his hand. "Take care of yourself. I'll be praying for you," she whispered, then left the room before giving in to the urge to kiss his forehead.

Saturday, 1:13 p.m.

"Ugh! Why is this so hard?" Kaymar pushed back from the table. She had spent the last evening and the majority of the morning surfing pet adoption websites without satisfaction. Inventory was not the problem; her indecisiveness constructed a wall she could not tear down. All of the dogs were cute and would make a good companion. Kaymar just didn't know if she wanted a Chihuahua or a Labrador Retriever. Just when she settled on one, another one would catch her attention. If she didn't decide soon, another Saturday would be lost cooped up in her unit. She'd already missed the farmer's market.

Truth be told, she wasn't sure she really wanted a dog, but she had to do something to redirect her focus. The past week was an emotional storm, and it really shouldn't have been. Caring for patients was her job. Her patients were something she left behind once she exited the parking lot. Until Jamal Turner. Mentally, Kaymar had tucked him deep inside and carried him everywhere she went. She woke up with thoughts of his well-being and drifted to sleep imagining how his voice sounded. The more she learned about him, the more she wanted to know. This attraction was not normal.

"Why did that even cross my mind?" She shook her head in disgust every time the thought of kissing him returned. It was just the forehead, but kissing a patient anywhere was unthinkable. What if she'd given into her urge and one of his family members saw? They already considered her time spent with him abnormal. She could lose her job. Jamal Turner wasn't worth losing her source of income. Whatever this thing was with him, it had to end now. If a canine companion didn't bring a resolution, divine intervention would. "Prayer changes things," she declared, while shutting down her computer.

Set on praying the *Jamal thing* away, Kaymar blasted worship music and quoted scripture the rest of the day. During the night, when thoughts of Jamal resurfaced, she prayed fervently for sleep. Sunday morning during worship service, Kaymar went to the altar for special prayer reinforcement from the prayer team. To enhance the detox, Kaymar stopped praying for Jamal's recovery. Enough prayers had gone up from her. Plus, she reasoned, he had his family. By Sunday evening, a calm she equated to peace enveloped her. She was delivered, set free of Jamal Turner's spell. She slept like a baby and woke up Monday morning feeling refreshed and renewed. At least for now.

Monday, 3:03 p.m.

"Do the best you can and try not to work too hard. Be sure to take your breaks and eat," April admonished the team after handing out shift assignments. "Let me know if there's anything I can help you with." Over the weekend, the ICU census increased, requiring each nurse to balance two patients.

Monica smirked. "Great. Just what I need after a weekend of ziplining, parasailing, and partying."

Kaymar scanned her assignment sheet and thought to tell Monica to plan her weekends with less activities but couldn't find her voice. As April advised, she had two patients – one heart attack and one stroke, but no comatose patient. No Jamal. Her feigned peace and deliverance evaporated leaving her more bound and twisted than before. All that prayer, reciting, and singing went out the window.

Trying to camouflage the sudden emptiness, Kaymar caught up with April before she rounded the nurse's station. "Do you know what happened to my patient that was in Bed D? Mr. Turner, the comatose patient? Did he wake up? Or did he..." Kaymar stopped speaking before the storm brewing within erupted. She needed to know and was terrified of knowing. If Jamal didn't make it...

An unreadable expression veiled April's face. "Oh, I forgot to tell you, he was transferred to the step-down unit. Yesterday, I think."

"Thank, God." Kaymar exclaimed before remembering April was an atheist. "I mean that's great."

April chuckled and patted her shoulder. "Don't worry about it. I know how close you were with him and his family. From what I remember, he's not out of the woods yet, but he is improving. Now go and work some of that healing power on your new patients."

"Sure."

Kaymar's steps back to the nurse's station weren't lighter. Her legs felt like lead. Anxiety gave her body a slight tremor. She needed to focus on her new patients, but she wanted to be with her former patient. The past battling with the present. As conflicted as she was, Kaymar had to push Jamal Turner out of her mind. And, as much as she hated to admit, her heart. *My heart? How did he get in there?*

"This is for the best," she mumbled, signing on to the EMR. "I need to stop cold turkey with this twisted infatuation. Maybe my prayers are being answered. I shouldn't have allowed myself to get attached to a patient, anyway. This is for the best." She recited those five words at least one hundred times throughout the night.

Every down moment was spent warring with her conscious about calling the step-down unit to inquire about Jamal. No longer his nurse, Kaymar did not have access to his EMR, and she'd be placing her job in jeopardy viewing a patient's record she was not currently giving direct care to. By end of the shift, her stroke patient had coded, and the heart attack patient succumbed. Kaymar was exhausted both mentally and physically. And she was hungry. There had been too much happening for a lunch break.

Not bothering to change into street clothes, she grabbed her jacket and gloves from the locker room. Every step to the car was heavier than the one before. Her shoulders slumped. Her feet ached, and her head throbbed. All of which had nothing to do with the shift she'd just completed. She paused long enough to ask her reflection in the driver side window, "What have you done? And how do you get out of it?"

Tuesday, 2:38 p.m.

Kaymar rode the elevator with new courage. After a good night's sleep, thanks to a double-dose of NyQuil, she was refreshed and determined to move past this emotional hiccup. She'd made the mistake of becoming attached to a patient, maybe even romantically interested, but she would get over it and move on. She would survive. In fact, she spent the morning singing the words to the Gloria Gaynor classic. She was still singing when she stepped off the elevator. The lyrics hung in her throat. Olivia Turner was walking toward her.

"Kaymar, I'm so glad I caught you before you started your shift. I've been hovering around this elevator for a half-hour, hoping to grab you for a minute." Anxiety and worry covered her face.

"Mrs. Turner, I mean Olivia." Kaymar stuttered. "What can I do for you?" Prayers for Jamal resumed without a warning. *Please let him be okay.*

"You have to come and see Jamal. Those nurses aren't treating him half as good as you did. Truth be told, I don't think they know what they're doing."

Kaymar breathed a sigh of relief. Jamal's condition hadn't worsened. "Is he awake?" She hoped her excitement didn't show.

"Oh yes! He woke up Sunday morning, mumbling something. He remembers the assault, which is good. The doctor and nurses tell me he's improving and will be back to normal soon, but I don't trust them like I do you. You have to come check on him at least once, so I'll have peace of mind," she persisted.

Kaymar failed at suppressing her pleasure in knowing Jamal had regained consciousness. She prayed her smile didn't reveal her distorted interest in her former patient. "I'm so happy Jamal has regained consciousness. And I pray he recovers completely, but I can't tend to a patient on another floor that I am not assigned to.

"Can you at least stop in on your break? He's in room 7204."

Olivia was smiling. What happened to the worry and anxiety from a moment ago? Kaymar didn't have time to find out. "Olivia, I can't promise anything. I have to change for work and don't know what my patient load will be." She started walking. "I'm sure Jamal is receiving the best of care. Please say hello to the rest of your family." Kaymar picked up speed and turned the corner before Olivia could rebut her dismissal.

Kaymar hated being rude, but she had to move on. She chalked up her attraction to Jamal as a byproduct of her lonely, boring life – which she was finally able to admit. She had used him for pseudo companionship because being comatose made him safe, but she hadn't planned on entangling her heart. Now that he was awake, there was no way she would cling to him like a lost puppy. If Kaymar had her way, no one in the Turner clan would ever see her again.

Friday, 2:31 p.m.

Kaymar strolled from her car to the garage elevator with purpose. Just eight more hours and the work week would be over. She'd made it through, heavy heart and all. Aside from losing two patients and playing hide-and-seek from the Turner clan, she'd had a good week, not counting her constant state of emotional turmoil. For three days, she got off the elevator on the floor above hers and took the back stairs down to ICU to avoid any possible run-ins with Olivia. Once, she spotted Mr. Turner in the cafeteria buying dinner and dashed out the side door without buying food. Yesterday, she saw Jamal's sister waving frantically in her direction as she walked through the parking garage. Kaymar responded by pulling out her cell phone and pretending to be engrossed in a conversation. She zigzagged between cars and hid behind a SUV until the woman was out of sight. Twice, she started up the stairs to

Jamal's floor and retreated back. She was officially on the rebound from whatever this thing with Jamal was. She vowed never again to allow her miserable life to interfere with her work again.

"Hey, Kay, hold the elevator," echoed against the cement walls.

Kaymar turned and mumbled, "Oh great." Thanks to the slow elevator, the motor mouth of the west would ride up with her. Ironically, Kaymar didn't mind if Monica ran off at the mouth today. Anything to redirect her thought.

"Hi, Monica," she managed with a manufactured happy face once Monica stepped inside the elevator nearly out of breath. "What's on the agenda for this weekend? You know I live my life vicariously through you," she lied.

If nothing else, Monica was predictable. With lightning speed, she poured out her weekend plans which included flying to Los Angeles for a concert, rock-climbing, and a hot-air balloon ride.

Kaymar held the manufactured smile and nodded. If only I were half as adventurous as this girl.

"Ooh, let me show you the video from the skydiving trip. The view was breathtaking." Monica pulled out her cell phone and started the video just as the bell for their floor chimed.

Kaymar leaned close to Monica and followed her off the elevator, forgetting her new ritual of stopping on the floor above.

"Wow!" Kaymar exclaimed. Monica was right, the view was spectacular. She took the phone from her. "I am way too scared to ever try that."

The two continued down the corridor with Kaymar singing a chorus of oohs and ahhs as Monica played video tour guide.

"Kaymar."

Kaymar's leg muscles instantly locked, immobilizing her. The breath she was about to expel lodged in her throat then reversed back into her lungs. She had to bend over to force the air out. A warm achy sensation filled her chest cavity. Involuntary reflex sent her free hand to her chest, but she didn't turnaround.

"Hey, are you okay?" Monica helped her maneuver upright. "What happened? You didn't get motion sickness from the video, did you?" She giggled.

Kaymar wanted to tell her how stupid that sounded but couldn't form words. And no, she was not alright.

"Kaymar," the voice from behind sounded again, this time more urgent.

This can't be happening. Sweat moistened her hands, and the phone slipped to the floor. She didn't have to turn around to know who the voice belonged to. The tenor voice was everything she'd imagined it would be – warm, yet strong with gentleness and a little sexy sprinkled in. And her name sounded divine flowing off his lips. *This really can't be happening. Why didn't I just get a dog?* She picked up the phone and handed it to Monica.

"I think that guy back there in the wheelchair is trying to get your attention."

Kaymar licked her lips and rubbed her hands together. "I know," she acknowledged. Instead of turning around, she continued her trek to the locker room.

Olivia yelled, "Kaymar, don't you run from us!"

Kaymar stopped.

"Do you know how hard it was for me to convince the nurse to let me push him around in this wheelchair, and then sneak him down here on a chance we'd run into you?" Olivia fussed. "You better get over here before security catches up with us."

You can do this. He's just a patient. The pep talk didn't work. Who am I kidding? I like this guy. Her body remained frozen.

"Do I need to call security," Monica asked.

"No. That's my comatose patient from last week and his mother. They're harmless." She heard movement, no doubt the wheelchair was getting closer. Time to face the music. "You go ahead, I'll meet you at report."

Monica looked over her shoulder. "Are you sure? Let give you my stun gun." She reached into her bag, but Kaymar stopped her.

"That's not necessary. They're just excited about Jamal's recovery. It'll only take a minute." If only it was that simple.

Monica repositioned the bag strap on her shoulder and shrugged. "If you say so. See you at report."

Monica continued on and Kaymar summoned the courage to face the conscious version of Jamal Turner.

"If I didn't know any better, I'd think you were avoiding me," Olivia continued. "I've been trying to catch you for days to get you to come up and see him. He's been asking about you since he woke up. His first word was— "

"Mother," Jamal interrupted. "I'll take it from here."

"Well, hurry up, before they come looking for us." Olivia yielded.

The authoritative voice nearly made Kaymar's knees buckle. Who was Jamal Turner? And what did Olivia mean, he's been asking about her?

"Kaymar, I don't mean to bother you, but I just had to meet the woman who changed my life before I leave the hospital tomorrow."

Curiosity got the best of her. "What are you talking about?" She spun around. "I was just doing my job. I—" The rest of the words hung in her throat. The up-close conscious Jamal Turner was far more appealing than the comatose patient. With the facial swelling and discoloration completely gone, his dark chocolate skin was smooth and even. Just as she'd imagined, dark brown eyes were shielded by those thick lashes. His teeth were both straight and white. The man was gorgeous and dangerous for her.

"Doing your job, as you put it, has left a lasting impression on me. You're a remarkable young woman."

Kaymar was so removed from the dating scene, she couldn't tell if Jamal was sincere or just spitting game. Either way, she thought the line was lame. She stopped gawking and folded her arms. "What lasting impression? You were in a coma? Remarkable? You don't know anything about me."

"I don't know much. Just that your name is Kaymar Washington. I won't say your middle name because you don't like it."

Kaymar gasped.

"Your favorite colors are orange and purple, but you're too conservative to wear them together. You drive a Honda, but your dream car is a Mercedes. You like to take long walks on the beach, but you don't know how to swim. You like old-school skates with the four wheels, but you're afraid to ride a bike because you fell and injured yourself when you were seven. You love spicy Mexican food and plan to start an organic garden this spring. You prefer romantic comedies over action movies. You've seen your favorite movie, *Pretty Woman*, over a hundred times. You love reading romance - historical romance being your favorite. The perfect Valentine's Day gift for you would be a box of *See's* dark chocolates, multicolored carnations, and a bottle of Juicy Couture. You love to pray and have a beautiful singing voice. You drown yourself in work because you don't want the hassles that come with relationships. You spend Friday and Saturday nights alone, but on Saturday mornings you enjoy volunteering at the food bank occasionally."

Kaymar's hands flew to her opened mouth. "Oh my God, you could hear." Her cheeks burned, and her head dropped in embarrassment.

"Yes. I heard everything you said. The first time you called my name sparked a desire in me to wake up. It was your voice that encouraged my soul. It was so sincere, like you really cared about my well-being. If that's your normal, then your patients are truly blessed."

"I usually don't divulge all my personal business to comatose patients. I've really got to get a life," she added, rubbing and shaking her forehead.

"Hopefully, this doesn't sound lame, but I really can't explain it any other way. Your voice gave me life. I think I began to depend on hearing your voice in my unconscious state. I don't even know if that's possible, but I needed to hear you say my name. I needed to hear you talk to me. I think that's why I woke up. I became agitated when I no longer heard your voice. Mama said I started moving fitfully and mumbling your name as I woke up."

Kaymar's head snapped up. "What?" How could a comatose man develop feelings for her? Jamal Turner had some serious game.

"And he's been asking for you every day since." Olivia added.

"Mother, please," Jamal pleaded, looking up at Olivia. "Let me finish."

"Okay. But hurry up before we get caught." Olivia turned away.

Jamal directed his attention back to Kaymar. "Honestly, I don't know what is happening, but I believe a divine connection has caused our paths to cross for a reason. I feel drawn to you, and from what my family tells me, I would venture to say you feel the connection."

"She most certainly does." Olivia was back. "I didn't buy that patient care crap for a second. Especially after your face fell when I mentioned his ex-wife. You're just as drawn to him as he is to you. That's why you've been hiding all week. I think this could be the beginning of a beautiful relationship," she added, then folded her arms and smiled.

"Mother, thank you for your commentary. Now, please let me finish."

Olivia threw her hands up. "Fine."

Irrational thoughts and emotions from anticipation to confusion to raw fear collided in Kaymar's being. *God, what is happening to me?* She wanted to scream, but her mouth just hung. Were her prayers for deliverance being mocked, or was her attraction to Jamel divinely orchestrated? She needed to check the latest medical journals to see if it was medically possible for Jamal to have heard and remembered all that stuff.

"As I was saying, Kaymar. Now that I'm awake, I would like to get to know you. To find out where our connection leads." A mischievous smile appeared. "And, now that I've physically met you, I'm certain there's a definite purpose for our paths crossing."

Kaymar couldn't hold the blush nor did she want to. The fact that Jamal found her attractive pleased her.

"We're having a small get together Sunday afternoon. Nothing formal or fancy, just family and friends to celebrate my recovery. I would love for you to come by, even for a little while. We can talk and hang out." He extended a piece of paper with his left hand. "Here's my phone number and the address. Please tell me you'll come."

How was Kaymar supposed to turn him down? His invitation was given with such sincerity and a handsome smile. Honestly, she didn't want to decline. If God was moving in her life, who was she to interfere? There was definitely something beyond her control drawing her to him. It was obvious she didn't know what or who was best for her. If Jamal was a fake, she would know soon enough. Tonight, she would begin her prayer by asking God about Jamal's role in her life. She took the paper and stuffed it in her pocket.

"I have to get to work," she said, looking at her wristwatch. "I'm glad you've recovered." She trotted off.

"Will I see you, again?" Jamal called after her.

Kaymar stopped briefly and graced him with a smile. "Yes, Jamal Turner. You will see me on Sunday."

Jamal's 'hallelujah' echoed down the corridor and into her heart.

About the Author

Wanda B. Campbell resides is the San Francisco Bay Area with her family. She proudly balances the roles of wife, mother, grandmother, minister, mentor, teacher, author, public health care worker, and college student. Wanda began writing in 2006, and currently has 12 published Christian Fiction novels. She has appeared on multiple best-selling lists and won various recognitions for her nontraditional edgy writing style. Wanda's passion is motivating others to fulfill their dreams and to pursue their passion. Learn more about Wanda's work at: wandabcampbell.com or join her Facebook group: Wanda B. Campbell Readers and Supporters.

Love Knows My Name

Dancing on the Moon
Linda Leigh Hargrove

When the TV news vans showed up at Carver High, I wanted to hide. The last time I'd been on camera, things had not turned out well.

The sixth period bell rang, and I stood glued to my spot behind my desk. All my eleventh grade pre-Calc students had already rushed to the windows, ogling the camera crews like this was their day to be on *The Voice*.

Dion Thomas turned to me. The young man was all smiles as he pulled a hair brush from his backpack. "Dr. Katrina, how do I look?"

I gave him my best droll expression. His hair was perfect. It was always perfect. His father, Principal Thomas, made sure of that. To be honest, Principal Nate Thomas took perfection to a new level with his tailored suits and fine manner.

Dion continued primping in the mirror app on his cell phone. Typical Dion Thomas. One of my brightest students but he tended toward the dramatic. A couple of the girls, his fan club, snickered as Dion started brushing the sides of his box fade.

"My hair alright?" he asked. "I want to look good on camera."

I started gathering my things into my briefcase. "Class, you are free to go. Did you not hear the last bell? I'm sure your bus drivers are not going to wait for you."

"There's my bus driver right there talking to one of the camera crews," one girl pointed out. "Check it. The news people are here for the charity dance, but it looks like everybody's trying to get a snap."

Dion slung his backpack over one shoulder and headed for the door. "Yep. And I'm ready for my close-up."

His fifteen fellow classmates grabbed their things and followed Dion out of my classroom, chatting him up as they went. And likely posting to Snapchat, no doubt.

"You coming, Dr. Katrina?" someone yelled out.

"Yeah, sure." I stammered. "Go on without me. I'll be there."

The conversation about the dance reminded me that I had yet to respond to the principal's email requesting chaperones. My new boss would not be happy about that. Even though I had only been on the job three months, I was expected to participate in school social events. Did each event have to involve cameras though?

The Valentine's Day Charity Dance had been Dion's brainchild. A fact that surprised me when I first found out. The proceeds benefited chronically-ill children at the local hospital. From what he'd told me in one of his more serious moments, his baby sister died of a rare heart malfunction when she was ten years old.

Encouraged by the football coach, Dion had started a service project for the hospital in his first year as one of the mighty fighting Carver Cardinals. That initial food drive turned into the charity dance. In its second year, the dance was completely led by students at Carver. They affectionately called it the Moon Ball because his sister's nickname had been Moon, for the way she loved the planets and stars.

I took another look out the window. My students had joined the throng outside. Someone had produced a large paper banner with Moon Ball in big letters painted across it and started a chant. I paused to listen. It was the first stanza of the song *Blue Moon*.

Another camera crew pulled up.

Why so many cameras?

I couldn't be on the news. That just wouldn't do.

My ex-boyfriend Jordan Banner knew I was no longer in Chicago, but he didn't need to know I was working at a high school in Raleigh, North Carolina.

Not that I was embarrassed about my new career choice. When Principal Thomas offered me the job three months ago, I was pleasantly shocked. Living in the South and working in a school with a high number of inner-city kids had been an adjustment, but my job was rewarding.

And there was also the joy of having Mr. Nathaniel J. Thomas as a boss. That was definitely a nice job perk. His leadership brought large amounts of talent and money into the neighborhood. And, he was easy on the eyes.

A knock on the door brought my thoughts back to the present.

Assistant Principal Ernie Goode leaned against the door frame. "Typical Dr. Katrina Mason. The first to arrive and the last to leave. You really work too hard."

I smiled. *He* was the one who was working too hard. Where Nate Thomas was debonair and respectable, Mr.

Goode was brash and annoying. Times ten. No wait. Times ten-thousand.

Thankfully, he had never gotten handsy with me. My ex's hands-on treatment had forced me to quit my tenure-track appointment at the University of Illinois at Chicago. Jobless and spineless, I'd moved as far away from my Chicago and UIC roots as I dared go.

I should have seen the writing on the wall when Jordan's occasional verbal jabs turned into abuse, but I stayed telling myself he would change. Thank the good Lord for teaching my hands to war. A girl can learn a lot of self-defense in ten months.

Ernie took a couple steps into the room. "You look nice today."

My mind went to the handwritten note in my briefcase.

"Trina, Be my Valentine. Can you dance for me at the Moon Ball?"

My first thought was to go to Assistant Principal Goode with the note. But then I realized Ernie Goode was the writer of the note. Somehow, he'd discovered my old stage name, Trina. I'm not sure how, but one thing was certain. Mr. Goode was bad news.

If I reported him to anyone at Carver, I'd probably have to admit my past indiscretions. My parents had eventually forgiven me for the part-time job I'd resorted to while a grad student at UIC, but I wasn't sure about Mr. Thomas. Though he looked to be in his late thirties, he was a strict man. And if he treated his employees like he treated his students, I'd be out on my ear in a heartbeat if he found out about my old "dancing" skills.

I'd have to figure out another way to deal with Mr. Goode. Positioning my keys in between my fingers, I pasted on a fake smile and faced Ernie Goode. He was going to let me out of this room the easy way or the hard way.

It's go time, Katrina.

"Of course, you always look nice," he added, looking at my feet.

It being Valentine's week, I'd worn my red pumps. A graduation gift from Mama. Silly me.

Fine Mr. Thomas hadn't said a thing about my shoe game. All I'd gotten out of him in the morning bus line was a curt nod and a smile. The same greeting he gave everybody.

There was a time when I had men hanging on my every move. But that was my former self.

Old things are passed away. All things have become new.

I took a breath and repeated my daily affirmation verse to myself as I strode forward. "We'd better join the others," I told Mr. Goode.

He let me pass without incident. Though I'm sure he took his time examining my backside.

The sound of footsteps drew my attention to the right as I exited my room.

"Hello, Dr. Mason," a woman's voice sang out.

Smiling, I greeted the principal's assistant with a side hug. "Hello, Mrs. Warren."

Our boss was two long-legged steps behind Mrs. Warren. He and I acknowledged each other with a polite bob of the head.

Mrs. Warren released me and started walking toward the outer doors. "I knew you were still in your room. Didn't I say that, Principal Thomas?"

"Yes, Leticia. You did."

Nate Thomas' deep voice reverberated through the hallway as he brought up the rear. "I noticed neither of you ladies have signed up to help chaperone the Moon Ball on Friday. The dance is in two days. But if we don't have enough teachers there, I don't mind cancelling it."

"We hear you, Mr. Thomas," Leticia Warren said, wagging a finger toward the ceiling. "I signed up today. Things have been busy with preparations for the Black History Month planning, but I did manage to put my name on the list during fifth period."

"I stand corrected. Thank you, Mrs. Warren. Dr. Mason, what's your excuse?"

"Umm ..." I came up empty under Nate Thomas' expectant glare.

He gave me a tight-lipped smile. "I'd really like you to come, Katrina."

Oh goodness. Why did he have to say my name like that? He'd only called me by my first name once before, during the school assembly we held after MLK Day. He'd accidentally stepped on my foot while approaching the podium. With a touch to my shoulder, he apologized for it. I hadn't felt a thing, but his gesture of concern sent me to cloud nine.

"Nathaniel James Thomas," Leticia scolded him like a big sister. "You're sounding more like your father every day."

Nate wagged his head. "Thank you for the reminder that I don't measure up, Auntie Letty."

He reached around Letitia and I as he pushed the outside door open for us. The chilly February air gushed past my bare legs.

"Ernie," Nate said, "Can I talk to you for a minute?"

I glanced over my shoulder at Ernie. The look on the man's face was priceless.

Gotcha, dude.

"I'll catch up with you ladies in a few," Nate called after us.

When the door slammed behind us, Letitia Warren leaned closer to me. "He likes you. Nate, that is. He plays the Officer McGruff role with all the new teachers."

"I hope you're right about that one."

"I know him well."

"I've heard him call you auntie before. I hope you don't mind me asking. Are you his aunt?"

"I don't mind at all, honey." Leticia tucked a lock of wavy black hair behind her ear. A few silver strands winked in the sunlight. "I'm fifteen years his senior. Used to babysit him when he was in Kindergarten. We grew up in this neighborhood. Course back then, it was a rougher place." I followed her gaze to the refurbished apartments across the street. What was once Section 8 housing was now high-dollar loft townhouses. I lived in one of them. High rise office buildings loomed in the distance.

Leticia went on. "You really should get more involved with the students, honey. They love you too, you know. Even though you're from up North, you fit right in. Please, come to the dance. You might even get old sourpuss Nate Thomas to cut the rug."

I laughed out loud. "The day I dance with old sourpuss will be the day I dance on the moon."

Leticia Warren's eyebrows inched up and a sly grin spread across her face. "Oh really? Dancing on the moon? Really? He is a good-looking man, don't you think?"

"That didn't come out right," I gushed. "What I meant to say was —"

She cut me off. "Dancing on the moon? Is that kind of like dancing on the ceiling? Remember that old Lionel Richie tune."

Leticia started clapping and humming a tune that sounded more like Richie's *All Night Long*.

"Hello, ladies," Nate said as he approached Leticia and I. Ernie was nowhere in sight. "Why are you humming *All Night Long*, auntie?"

Leticia stopped clapping. Her smile turned upside down.

Principal Thomas looked at me. His eyes were narrowed. Hard lines of concern marked his face.

To my left, I heard Leticia take a sharp breath. "Welp, I'd better go see what that Dion is up to. Cutting up for the cameras no doubt." She waggled her finger in the air and spoke over her shoulder as she left. "The news people will want a statement from you too, Principal Thomas. Don't be long."

"I won't be long, Mrs. Warren."

He unbuttoned his suit coat and placed his hands on his hips. A warm spicy aroma enveloped me as he leaned closer. Ominous but inviting at the same time. Oh my word, did this man smell good or what?

I studied the tips of my red shoes. "Am I in trouble, Principal Thomas?"

"No. Not this time. But I am upset."

I forced myself to look into his eyes.

"I put Ernie on fifteen days leave without pay while he gets some workplace sensitivity training. It took me a while to figure out what he was doing to you. Actually, it was Auntie Letty who brought it to my attention."

I could have run over and kissed the woman.

"I wonder how many other pretty women he's harassed on this property. Why didn't you tell me?" He shook his head and held up a hand. "Strike that. I know I can be standoffish sometimes. I do care about ... about my staff."

The warmth in his eyes made my heart skip a beat.

His staff.

"Of course," I said, my voice barely above a whisper.

He touched my shoulder briefly and my heart completely stopped.

"I want you to know that I'm sorry this happened. I feel responsible—"

"No, please ... I should have come forward. Thank you for handling it."

"No one will have to know anything. Okay?"

"Okay," I said finding my voice again.

With a sweep of his hand, he changed the subject. "So, if helping chaperone the dance is out of the question for you, can I twist your arm to help us beautify the campus for the Black History Month program next week?"

Up ahead, one of the teachers was waving for us to move closer to the camera crews. It seemed Principal Thomas was up next.

"I saw that in your email," I said. "The time escapes me though. Remind me when that is again."

"This afternoon, actually. In about an hour. We have a group of JROTC kids helping too but ..." He cast a glance to the apartments across the street. "I figured since you lived nearby and most of the other teachers are already signed up to chaperone."

"Share the load," I said, repeating one of the school's credos. "Sure, I'll come."

"Excellent," he beamed. "You are a wonderful asset to our teaching team, Dr. Mason. Thank you." He took a few strides toward the camera crews then turned to me again. "See you back here at 4pm."

Reflecting on my day, I entered my apartment and changed into sweats. I realized something. Good-looking, long-legged Nate Thomas had called me pretty.

My heart took wings.

* * *

The Junior ROTC students showed up in their drab olive-green t-shirts and camouflage pants carrying rakes, shovels and bags of mulch. Their student commander had no instructions for me and didn't know when I could expect Principal Thomas.

While she and her squad continued raking errant piles of leaves, I checked my watch for the umpteenth time.

4:16pm.

No sign of Nate Thomas.

"You've been stood up," I told myself as I pushed off the curb and grabbed my dollar store gardening gloves. "Time to go home."

Home wasn't too far away. In fact, I could see it from where I stood. My tuxedo cat, Harry, sat in the window swishing his tail left and right.

"I miss you too, Harry."

A car came to an abrupt stop a few feet away. I waved at the two people sitting in the front seat. Dion leaned out the driver's side and yelled my name.

"Hold that thought, cat," I said, speaking to my feline flat mate.

I waited for Nate and Dion to approach. Nate carried two long trays of potted flowers.

"Sorry we're late," Nate said. "Between the teenage driver and a run on flowers at the neighborhood garden center…"

Dion chuckled. "Don't blame me. I was driving as fast as I could."

"I know. My heart was in my throat."

"Yeah. Yeah." Dion drifted toward the JROTC students working across the schoolyard. "Dad, do you mind if I go help them?"

"No, I don't mind." Dion trotted off. Nate placed the flowers on the curb beside my feet. "He's sweet on the JROTC commander. Wants to invite her to the Moon Ball. With those cute freckles of hers, she's bound to already have a date."

"Cute freckles?" The words slipped out before I could stop myself.

I self-consciously touched my face.

No one had ever described freckles as cute. My former boyfriend had always warned me about getting too much sun because exposure made my freckles multiply. A high-yellow sister with freckles did not fit into his family's lifestyle. With their summer cottage in Oak Bluffs near Dr. Henry Louis Gates' and a box at the Civic Opera House, the girl from the south side of Chicago was probably not their first choice for their only son.

But Principal Thomas liked freckles. I bit my lip to hide the giddy feeling bubbling up inside.

Nate looked away. "Sorry. I spoke out of turn, Dr. Mason. I'll stick to flowers." He grabbed the trays of flowers and headed toward the planter boxes near the front entrance. "This way."

I pulled up alongside him, walking twice as fast to keep up with his long stride. "You know, Nate, you really don't have to call me Dr. Mason now. I'm not that stuck on myself."

Nate plopped the trays down on the pavement beside the planters. "I think you should be proud of your accomplishments. You're not proud of your degrees?"

"I'm not ashamed of my education. I just don't want any special treatment."

"Fair enough." He stooped down and brushed his hand across the tray of flowers. "This afternoon, you're just one of the team. A fellow grunt."

The yellow and purple petals of the flowers trembled in the breeze. I let out what I thought was a manly grunt and kneeled beside him. He chuckled.

The afternoon sunshine felt good on my skin. "It turned into such a glorious day."

"Yeah, it's weird really. Considering we had six inches of snow two weeks ago. You're not in Chicagoland anymore. That's for sure." He patted the flowers on the tray. "Now, we have thirty-six of these little purple babies. These two trays and more in the trunk of my car. We'll put most of them here in this bed and the rest in the planters near the front door. Do you mind doing the front door planters by yourself? Divide and conquer?"

I stammered for a few seconds then finally decided to come clean. "I have a confession. I've never planted flowers before."

He grinned. "Tell you what, I can teach you. Me and Dion usually do the extra grounds beautification by ourselves, above and beyond the groundskeeping the school district provides. It's easier than it looks. As long as you don't snap their heads off, these pansies are pretty hardy."

I watched in awe as his long fingers tenderly coaxed the flowers, dirt and all, from their little plastic pots.

He cradled the roots in the palm of his hand. "I'm glad to see you've got gloves. I'd hate for you to mess up your nice nail job."

"I'm not a prissy girl, you know."

"Says the woman who wears bright red pumps to school."

"Oops." I giggled. "Sorry. They're really quite comfortable."

"I'm sure they are. They're certainly hard to miss." He shifted the plant to his left palm and broke off the bottom inch or so of dirt from the wad of roots. "This baby was a little root bound."

"Root bound?"

"Yep." He placed the flower on the bed and lifted another from the tray. "Let me show you. You're right handed so, hold it in your left palm. Gently but firmly. Don't squeeze."

He supported my left hand with his own. The heat from his fingers was unsettling and delicious at the same time. A second later, he released me and was scooping another plant from the tray.

"Watch me." He pinched off another bottom portion. "Just take off a small bit of that bottom. Don't worry if you break some roots in the process."

I tried it. The action made a soft snapping sound like I was breaking a handful of small twigs.

"You want to shock these wadded up roots into growing again," he said.

Shock the roots.

The thought gave me pause.

My roots, or foundation rather, had been shocked in the past year. Had it led to any growth for me?

No. Not a single bit. In many ways, it seemed like I had taken too many steps backward. I said my Bible promise scriptures each day, but I felt far away from Him. Work at the university and my relationship with Jordan had consumed me.

I sat back on my heels and looked at the little plant. It looked so perfect, with its little frilly purple leaves. Yet it was so vulnerable. With just a twist, I could snap off some bound roots or, if I went higher, I could pop off its head.

A goner.

Three months ago, I felt like a goner. Was I still a goner? Or was Carver High and Raleigh, NC, another chance? A permanent new start?

Please, Lord.

Nate's voice brought me back to the present. "Now, once you've broken off the bottom, line it up along the front edge of the flower bed like so." He placed the five plants he had prepared in the exposed earth of the bed, with a hand width between them. "Do the entire tray and then arrange them equidistant before digging the hole for it."

Nate continued talking about his flower babies.

If I was honest with myself, I felt like I was in the hole. Work at Carver was my only bright spot. When I left school, I slipped into a deep dark place all too quickly. Sure I had my cat and my affirmations. They lifted me out for a few rays of goodness, but it was so hard sometimes. The joy never seemed to last.

I stole a glance at my new boss. Strong. Confident. Talented. Multifaceted and seemingly content with what life had given him.

Why, with all my accomplishments, was I so empty? I stared at a divot in the soil.

Empty, like a hole.

I hung my head to hide the sadness. Taking another plant from the tray, I broke off the roots. Tears slid out to the ends of my eyelashes.

"Are you okay, Katrina?" Nate stood over me.

Sniffling, I used the cuff of my sleeve to wipe my nose.

He kneeled beside me and cupped my hands in his. His gritty palms were warm and soothing.

"I'm fine." I said, surrendering the plant to his gentle prompting.

"You're not. Talk to me. Why are you crying?"

"It's complicated."

He nodded. "Life can be." He placed my plant in the tray again and dusted off his hands. Standing, he urged me to do the same. "Let's take a short walk."

I brushed my hands on the front of my sweats and followed him.

"What do you do for fun, Katrina?"

"It's obvious I don't garden."

We laughed at my joke.

"I'm not picking on you," he said. "And just so you're wondering, planting flowers today isn't an extension of your job interview. This is team building but it's also friendship building. I would like to think my employees see me as a friend and an ally, not an enemy."

We stopped at the corner and waited for the walk light to change.

"Katrina, if there's anything you'd like to talk about... anything at all, please feel free to come to me. Promise me that. After what I discovered today about Mr. Goode, I wanted you to know that you and I are on the same team. You don't have to hide things from me. Promise?"

I forced myself to look into his face. I saw honesty and kindness and strength. "I promise."

"Good."

We walked to the end of a block where he pointed towards downtown. The Raleigh skyline glistened majestically in the setting sun.

"Most of our students come from this neighborhood around the school. Many of the whites who attend Carver are bussed in, but students like Dion grew up here. He spent the first ten years of his life here. I was his big brother. You know, like in the Big Brothers Big Sisters of America program? He was raised in this drug-infested neighborhood by a single mom. When she went to prison for possession, she allowed me to be his guardian. Eventually, I adopted him and changed his last name to match mine.

"He still sees her sometimes. Because of her early positive influence, he gives back to the neighborhood. Everything I know about plants and growing things came from that little boy through his mother who is now a recovering crackhead. She wasn't always broken, you see. So yeah, life is complicated."

"Wow. I had no idea."

"Yeah, not many people do. Roots can be so tangled." With that proclamation, he turned around and led the way back to Carver.

In that moment, I wanted to know more about him. And I also wanted him to know more about me.

"You're one deep individual, Mr. Thomas."

He shrugged. "Nah. Not really."

"Did you ever think about going for your Ph.D.?"

"Sure. For a hot minute."

"What changed your mind?"

"The time. The money. And one question ... What would I do with it? I'm already doing what I want to do with my life."

We returned to our flower bed project and worked side by side in silence. Occasionally, I'd hear him humming or muttering something to himself.

I felt safe with him. Who would have thought I'd be planting flowers in the middle of February with a big black man by my side? A man who, unlike my ex, thought a light-skinned black woman with freckles was pretty.

On top of that, it felt good to be needed. To be giving back. But it also felt good to know Nate Thomas a little better.

We washed our hands in the school bathroom and bid the JROTC crew farewell.

Dion wasted no time getting back in the car. "I'm headed over to Sammy's house. Is that all right, Dad?"

"Yeah. I'm cool with that. Home by nine."

Dion's shoulders sagged. "Nine o'clock?"

"You heard me, dude. Nine."

The boy sighed. "Gotcha, Dad. See you later, Dr. Mason."

"Goodbye, Dion."

We watched the teenaged driver peel off.

"How are you getting home?"

"Walking. We live about ten minutes that way." He pointed eastward. "Hope I didn't keep you out too long. I really appreciate your help. Let me walk you to your place."

He escorted me to the front door of my apartment building.

I took the key from my pocket and took a deep breath. "Actually, there was one thing I wanted to talk with you about."

"Uh oh." Nate grimaced. He looked a little like a disappointed Dion. "What did I do this time?"

"It's about Ernie Goode."

His grimace turned into a deep scowl.

"What will happen to him?"

"He'll get what he deserves. If it were up to me, he'd be fired. But I have to take it to the school board. You're an attractive unattached woman, but that gave him no right to stalk you the way he did."

I felt warm under his gaze.

Oh God, I'm blushing.

He stared down at me, probably noticing just how *cute* my freckles looked when my face turned red. When I looked up again, his eyes seemed to be focused on my lips.

I crossed my arms and stood as straight as I could. "Are you about to kiss me, Mr. Thomas?"

He averted his eyes and cleared his throat. "No, I was not. You ... uh ... you have a smudge of dirt on your chin. I think it's dirt. Though I'm not sure if it's dirt or a freckle."

Using the cuff of my sleeve I scrubbed at my jaw. The fabric came back smudged. "Did I get it all?"

"You missed some of it." He stepped toward me, and the anticipation of his touch made me tremble inside. When he brushed my chin with his fingers, my knees went weak.

"There," he said, his voice husky. "It was dirt after all. All gone now."

His hand lingered on my face, brushing my chin once more. His thumb touched my earlobe, and he looked at my lips again.

Did he mean to kiss me?

He drew a quick breath and blinked before snatching his hand away. "Goodnight, Dr. Mason. See you in school tomorrow."

* * *

Thursday was Valentine's Day. I went to work in black patent leather wedges, not red pumps, and kept a low profile. Dion, and his blessed green thumb, gave each of the women teachers a small potted plant to celebrate the day. To his JROTC sweetheart, he gave an African violet, which he presented with great fanfare at their lunch break. She blushed and kissed him on the cheek. The onlookers in the cafeteria, myself included, applauded. I was more than a little jealous.

The only Valentine gift I had received was a suggestive note from Ernie Goode.

I did not see my boss face to face at all during regular hours, although I did hear his booming voice in the hallway scolding a tardy student. While making copies in the main office during my planning period, I spied his office door ajar. But it wasn't like I was seeking him out.

So, I told myself.

Yesterday, I had wanted to kiss him. The vulnerable look in his eyes as he gazed into mine kept replaying in my mind all day. I was willing to let him kiss me... in that moment. First thing Thursday morning was a different story. A case of the *awkwards* afflicted me, and I quickened my pace when I passed his office.

"You're too old for this," I told myself as I packed up at the end of the day.

I had to talk to him. Get some things off my chest. Sit across the room, out of arms reach of course, and torment myself by looking deep into those big, expressive brown eyes of his.

Lord, help. I prayed silently as I marched past the last few students lingering in the halls after last bell.

I made my way to his office silently practicing what I'd say. I don't think this workplace romance is a good idea, Mr. Thomas.

No, that wouldn't do.

We didn't have a workplace romance. What we had was an almost kiss. Sort of.

I took a deep breath and pushed through the double-doored entry of the front office. The place was deserted. Nate's door was still partly open, but I didn't hear a thing. Mrs. Warren's desk, to the right of his door, was vacant. Her computer appeared to be shut down.

"Hello," I called out.

I heard a thud from Mrs. Warren's desk. Followed by a muffled oath.

The top of Leticia Warren's head appeared from behind her office chair. She was rubbing her ear.

I gasped, tossed my briefcase and purse on her desk, and rushed to her side. "Leticia, are you okay?"

With a pained expression on her face, she nodded. "I was picking up some money I dropped behind my chair when you startled me."

"I'm sorry." I helped her sit in her chair.

She shook it off. "I'll live. So, were you looking for Nate or his principal intern?"

"I didn't know he had an intern. I was looking for Nate."

"I figured as much. Nate, or should I say our Ghost Principal, has been incog-negro since lunch. Told me he had some urgent business at NC State today. Anything I can help you with?"

I shook my head.

Leticia stood and slipped her arms into a jacket. "I'll be heading out then." She stopped a moment and turned her head to one side as if she was considering something. "Do you have dinner plans, Dr. Katrina?"

I got my things from her desk. "Well ... uh ..."

"Come have Valentine's dinner with us. Every year Mr. Warren and I host a special dinner for the singles in our church." I followed her out of the office. "Have you found a good church home?"

I had not. Maybe that was what I was missing? Within the first six weeks of accepting my job at UIC, I had started going to a church on the Southside. At first, it was to spite Jordan, then it was because it felt good. Then, life got in the way.

I yearned for that feeling again.

"When is the dinner?"

"Six o'clock," she replied. "I'll text you my address. Can you bring a dessert? Nothing fancy. Store-bought will work. The mister and I will provide the main course."

My phone chirped signifying I'd received a new text message. "Sure thing. Thanks."

* * *

Mr. Warren was a jovial man with a salt and pepper afro and beard. He reminded me of Cedric the Entertainer in the *Barbershop* movie series. Minus the foul mouth, of course.

It was obvious that Larry Warren loved his wife, his goddess as he called her. According to Leticia, they had invited twelve singles from the church group. Two men and two women showed. I was the only one without a 'date,' but I didn't mind.

From the way one of the men made eyes with the little redhead woman, I could tell they were an item. Funny thing, that didn't make me uncomfortable. Sitting in that dining room with Nate Thomas ... now, that would have made things really uncomfortable.

"Too bad all the others couldn't make it," Mr. Warren said, slicing into the second apple pie. "But that means more pie for me. That was a lovely roast my goddess cooked for us."

"Thank you, darling," Leticia gushed. "Who wants coffee? Katrina, can you give me a hand in the kitchen?"

I lifted the stack of dirty plates from the center of the dining table and followed Leticia into the kitchen. "That was quite a dinner." I lowered the dishes down into the sink full of sudsy water.

"It's not over yet, honey. There's dessert and games."

"Games? Nice."

"And, let me warn you, Mr. Warren is very competitive. He likes to win."

I dipped my finger into a bowl of whipped cream and deposited the sweet dollop in my mouth. "Nothing wrong with wanting to win."

"Stop that, child. Get your finger out of that bowl. I declare, you are worse than Nathaniel."

Her mention of Nate made me a little self-conscious.

"I wonder what happened to that young man. I invited him. Emailed him. Texted him. I hope he and Dion are having a nice dinner together."

She hummed to herself as she filled cups of coffee. "I'm not trying to play matchmaker, dear heart. I hope you know that. I just didn't want you sitting at home alone on Valentine's Day."

I put up my hands in surrender. "I would never accuse you of such, Mrs. Warren."

"I've been accused of worse." Leticia nodded her head toward the counter. "Grab that little tray with the creamer and sugars, and I'll carry the tray with the cups. Thank you for your help."

"And thank you for inviting me."

"You're welcome, Katrina."

"Now, let the games begin," Mr. Warren announced when his wife and I reentered the dining room.

We ate apple pie and played Pictionary. An hour later, my jaws hurt from laughing at Mr. Warren's antics and bad drawing skills. In between the lively banter, the others talked about God's involvement in their lives like it was a natural thing to do. It made me feel good, but my uncertainty was also there. Did being involved in their fun also mean being open about my past? I was torn.

Around nine, the little red-haired girl announced she was heading home. It wasn't a surprise when her admirer volunteered to accompany her to her car. The other two members of the singles group started discussing plans for a trip later in the spring with the Warrens. Feeling like a huge fifth wheel, I gathered dessert dishes and wandered into the kitchen.

I washed the dishes to kill time while entertaining the thought of leaving. Then without so much as a knock, the back door opened and in walked Nate Thomas. He wore a red Carver Cardinal's hoodie over a white tee and looked more like a linebacker than a principal.

His mouth hung open for a few seconds, obviously shocked to see me in the Warren's kitchen.

"Hi," I said breaking the awkward silence.

"Hello, Katrina. I guess ... um ... I guess you came to the Valentine's dinner."

I nodded.

Laughter filtered in from the dining room.

The roasting pan sat on the island between us. Nate reached over, pinched off a piece of pot roast and popped it in his mouth. "Mmm, that's good. Leticia is a good cook. Did she make her famous rolls too?"

He lifted the dishtowel Leticia had draped over an empty bread basket and frowned.

"You should have come to dinner. She said she invited you."

"Yeah, she did. I had ... I had some business to take care of." He took another bite of pot roast. "No, honestly, that's a lie. Sort of. Well, I did have some things to do at State, but I could have made it to the dinner. The truth is I was avoiding you." He glanced my way and then looked out the window over the sink.

This shy Nate was intriguing.

He shoved his hands in his pockets. "I figured you were here. I was waiting in the backyard trying to gather my courage. Then I saw you through the window washing dishes just now." He gulped and let out a long breath. "I stepped out of line yesterday. When I tried to ... um ... you know ... after we planted flowers."

"When you almost kissed me?"

His eyes bugged. "Yeah that. That was unprofessional, and I'm sorry. You did have some dirt on your chin by the way." He paused and looked at my lips before averting his eyes again. "Well, like I said I'm sorry. Can you forgive me?"

My voice squeaked when I tried to respond. I cleared my throat and tried again. "I forgive you."

He stood there in silence for a few seconds twirling a ring on his pinky finger. If it wasn't for the way the shirt revealed the muscles of his chest and shoulders, I'd say he looked like a little lost and confused teenage boy who needed comfort.

My thoughts were wandering into dangerous territory. I needed to change the subject. "So how's Dion?"

Nate shrugged. "He's good. He and his girl went to the movies right after school." He chuckled. "Poor dude had to work tonight. Mr. Dion "Love" Thomas could not go out on Valentine's Day."

I laughed too. "You saw his show in the cafeteria today?"

"No, but he told me all about it. You know him. Didn't leave a single detail out."

"He's a good kid."

"Yeah, he is. Thanks for saying that. I wonder sometimes how good of a dad I am."

"You're a great dad."

He shrugged and twisted the pinky ring some more. "Thanks."

"What's that ring on your finger?" I secretly hoped it wasn't from a girlfriend.

"Oh." He glanced down at his hand. "I bought it for my daughter when we found out she was sick. She used to wear it on a chain around her neck as a way to always have me with her. She died several years ago. Wearing the ring helps me remember the good times we had."

How sad.

"So young. I'm sorry to hear that."

He shrugged and blinked several times. "Can we change the subject? I wish you would reconsider being a chaperone for the Moon Ball tomorrow night. Ernie can't come. So we're down one person."

"I'll come."

He beamed. "Thanks. You don't have to wear anything special."

"Aw shucks. I was hoping to wear my red shoes."

"Please do. I'll wear my tux."

I was impressed. "You have a tux?"

"Sure do. Got it on clearance." He swallowed hard and took a step closer to me. His voice was lower when he spoke. "Whatever happens tomorrow, I want you to promise me something."

Frowning, I shook my head. "What are you saying, Nate? What's going to happen tomorrow?"

The voices from the dining room got rowdier. I was certain Mr. Warren's guffaw could have been heard a block away. Were they playing games again? I felt torn. Go join in the fun or stay here with this gorgeous man. I felt safe with Nate Thomas, but the tone had turned serious, dangerous.

With a touch to my shoulder, Nate helped me make up my mind.

"Katrina, can you step out with me for a minute?" He looked me in the eye. I gulped. "I can tell from that look you think I'm up to something."

I put my hands on my hips. "Well, are you? Will you try to kiss me again?"

He turned to the side and let out a little growl. "Daggone it, woman. Did you have to bring that up again?" Stepping back, he looked at me again. "Listen,

I'm not going to try anything. I'm like Dion. We're both jocks. We think better while we're moving."

In one fluid motion, he stretched back and opened the kitchen door.

"After that personal defense thing you did yesterday with your crossed arms, I ain't messing with you, Katrina Mason."

I allowed myself a laugh. He smiled.

"Listen, Katrina, I just want to talk. To ask you a few things ... privately."

Eyeing the door, I drew a long breath. Is this where he asked me about my days as a stripper? Was I prepared to come clean about everything? If he asked me directly, I would be honest. Until then, I would not volunteer anything extra.

I tried to make eye contact, but he was looking down. Uh oh. As far as I was concerned, this was a sure sign that he knew something damning about me.

Time to face the music, Katrina Mason.

I took another deep breath and strode through the open door. Nate followed and pulled the door closed behind us.

The click of the door sounded loud in the chilly darkness. In the distance, a dog barked. Overhead, a fingernail sliver of a moon shone, offering very little light.

"The Man in the Moon is smiling tonight," Nate said as he walked down the back steps.

I turned my head sideways. "It does kind of look like a lopsided smile."

While I studied the heavens, Nate took off his hoodie and draped it over my shoulders. It swallowed me in warm softness.

"Thank you," I said.

"Watch your step," Nate cautioned as I descended to his level. "Leticia leaves treats for the stray cats in the neighborhood. Mr. Warren's dog has fits barking at them, and sometimes the cats leave treasures from their nighttime hunts on the steps."

Grossed out, I pulled out my cell phone and turned on the flashlight app. After making sure the steps were clear, I joined Nate on the grass. "Thanks for the warning. Harry brings me little dead gifts sometimes. When I let him out, I mean."

Nate spoke over his shoulder as he walked across the yard. "I'm hoping you're talking about a cat."

The comment made me giggle. "Yes, Harry is my cat."

In that moment, I wanted so much for our conversation to stay right there. To talk about cats and dead rats on doorsteps, but I knew we were walking through the Warren's yard in the dark for quite another reason.

Instead of talking right away, Nate continued his stroll past a little pergola in the center of the yard and toward the back fence. He unlatched a gate and invited me to walk through.

"You're killing me with this silence, Nate." I stepped to the other side and waited for him to say something. He didn't. "Am I about to lose my job?"

He shook his head. The frown on his face was very clear in the glare of the streetlight overhead. "No. No. Carver High can't afford to let you go." Once more, he twisted the ring on his little finger. "This is hard for me to ask."

"Let's walk then. Maybe it will help if we don't look at each other."

If I had to tell him about my past, I didn't want to look him in the eye.

"Good idea." He started walking and I followed. After a few steps, he started talking. "When I finished my undergrad in psychology, I thought God was leading me to go for my Master of Divinity degree. I got into Duke's Divinity School."

"Good for you. I hear it's hard to get in there."

"It is, but I blew it. I made some wrong turns. Got involved with the wrong woman at the wrong time." He paused and twisted the ring. "Anyway, we had a little girl together and I dropped out of Duke. Our baby was born sick. She had a deformity. I thought it was God's judgment on me for getting involved with a prostitute. But now I see it as God's grace."

Grace?

An odd word to use. I craned my neck to look into his face. He kept his head down and kept walking.

"I left God alone for a long time after that, but I'm glad He didn't leave me. While I worked odd jobs to support my daughter and her mom, I got my master's degree in instructional design and technology from State. Despite my best efforts to buy the right doctors, my daughter died. I was devastated. Once again, I tried to leave Him."

Nate stopped walking and tilted his face to the night sky. The moon sliver smiled down on us.

"He showers us with grace," Nate said. "At every turn, He showed me mercy. Favor. Goodness. Forgiveness. Restoration. He drew me closer. He brought me through all the years of training and preparation to become the principal, the man I am today. He gave me Dion as my Ebenezer."

Nate wiped his eyes and looked at me. "During your interview, you mentioned an Ebenezer."

"I did? Are you sure. I'm not even sure what that is."

"In Bible terms, it is a stone of help, a reminder of God's help and grace. The Israelites would place stones in the desert when something momentous happened as a reminder."

I searched my memory of the interview and came up empty. My nerves had been on edge, I suppose. It was all a blur.

Nate went on. "When I asked about your favorite color. You said it was red."

"Yes, I remember that."

"And you said it was because the color red reminded you of your alma mater but also of God's saving power and sacrifice for you."

My recollection returned. "And I said, when I got the call from you to interview to be a member of Carver Cardinal's family, I took it as a sign from God that I was heading in the right direction. Since your school colors are black, white, and red. I thought it was corny at the time."

"It wasn't corny. As the chair of the hiring committee, it was just what I needed to hear. In an interview, we can't ask much about a person's religious beliefs. We just sit there and pray for a reason to select or reject. You gave me a solid reason to select you with that statement. But I need to know more tonight, Katrina."

I drew a shaky breath. "So this *is* an extension of that interview? I thought you said —"

"Your job is not in jeopardy. You have my word on that. I need to know more. It's been on my mind since that day, but I didn't think it was my place to ask you but now ... now I need to know for sure."

Nate turned and looked at me directly.

"This is a yes or no question. Can you name a time, a place, a day when you made that decision to follow the Man who made the ultimate sacrifice for your life?"

Without a bit of hesitation, I answered. "Yes. Yes, I can. I keep that date in my Bible."

Tension bled from his body. "And when was that?

My mind went to the moonlit night in the club parking lot almost five years earlier. Unlike tonight, the moon was shining in full brilliance. I could clearly see the joy in the faces of those church ladies who gave me, a sinful woman, a gift basket full of fruit and money. They had been sending me gifts of food and toiletries for several weeks before that night.

Sadly, it was the gift of money that got my attention. That made me pause long enough to reexamine my life choices. They had taken me under their wings and walked with me through the first stages of growth in God. Helped me find scholarship money and self-respect.

Grace.

I clearly remembered the night I kneeled in that parking lot with those sweet sisters in Christ to accept God's gift of grace. "It was August 20, 2013."

A tear trickled down Nate's cheek. Laughing, he pulled me into a hug. "Thank you. Thank you."

"You're welcome," I replied, my answer muffled against his muscular shoulder.

The yapping of a little dog broke our embrace.

"Excuse me," came a familiar man's voice.

I turned around to see Mr. Warren holding a little fluffy dog on a leash. "Hi, Mr. Warren."

"Y'all ain't making out on this here sidewalk, are you?"

"No, sir," Nate said. "It was a hug. That's all."

Mr. Warren walked past, and his dog continued to yap at us. "Hug? Looked like some kind of slow drag dance to me. Better save that for the Moon Ball tomorrow night. See y'all there. Behave yourselves."

* * *

I wasn't looking forward to the Moon Ball, but every other member of the Carver Cardinals family was. The entry way of the school was decked out with Chinese lanterns and red paper cutouts. It looked like a late Chinese Lunar New Year celebration.

Red.

The color red was everywhere. Mingled with gold and yellow. It reminded me of my conversation with Nate last night. After he had walked me back to the Warren's house, I said goodnight to everyone and went home.

In the quiet of my townhome, I searched the scriptures for everything I could find about Ebenezers. Stones of help were in so many places. Why had I missed them before?

Throughout the day, my mind kept returning to the scriptures and to what Nate had shared about his life. Our paths crossed a couple times during the day, but he seemed distant.

Was he embarrassed about what he shared? After school, I dressed for the dance and decided I would tell him our friendship was still intact.

To be honest, I wanted more than friendship from the tall, dark and handsome man. But I guessed being his friend was better than nothing.

At 7:30, I heard the music from the dance through my closed bedroom window. Harry's meowed protests were comical.

"Don't be rude, cat," I told him. "I'm going to that party. It's for charity so be nice."

Two freshmen Junior Varsity football players met me at the gym door, which had been strung with tiny white Christmas lights.

The technology class had rigged a large disco ball in the center of the gym. Its sparkles were bouncing off all the walls and the small crowd gathering inside.

"Can I take your coat, Dr. Katrina?" one of the little football players asked me.

His teammate punched him in the arm. "Not 'can', dude. It's 'may'!"

I laughed at the grammar discussion as I slipped out of my faux fur stole. "Yes, you *may* take my wrap."

Junior Mr. Grammar gave me a coat check card and left me to my own devices. Mr. and Mrs. Warren found me standing by the punch bowl.

"Oh my goodness," Leticia exclaimed as she looked me up and down. "You are stunning. That's one hot little number."

I'd picked the dress, a satiny black sheath with spaghetti straps, with Nate's tux in mind. But I wasn't telling her that.

"Oh, this old thing," I said. "Thanks. You two look nice as well."

"Thanks, sweetie," Mr. Warren said. "Don't know where your hugging partner got to. He's around here someplace."

My hugging partner kept his distance for much of the dance. He and Dion, as it turned out, were co-emcees for the event. Every half hour, they turned the lights up a little and made an announcement from the stage about the funds raised for the hospital.

Grinning, Dion waved out over the crowded gym. "Hey, y'all. We're doing great. As of ten minutes ago, we've raised $10,453. That's amazing! And we still have two hours to go. So please keep posting to social media. And keep it clean, y'all. You're not only repping the mighty fighting Cardinals, you're also repping the kids of our generation. We can make a difference."

The students sent up a roar of agreement, and I clapped and cheered with them.

Someone touched me on the shoulder. I started and turned around. It was my boss, looking striking in his tuxedo and fresh haircut. Way better than my tuxedo cat.

Nate leaned closer and whispered in my ear. "I'm leaving Carver."

I laughed. "I'm sorry but it sounded like you said you're leaving Carver. Must be the loud music."

Smiling, he shook his head. "I've accepted a three-year position as a consultant for a project at NC State."

"You what?" I couldn't believe my ears.

The light around us shifted to cooler shades of white and blue. The music slowed. The students on the dance floor drifted closer and draped their arms around each other, swaying slowly to the beat.

I repeated my question. "You're leaving Carver? Why? Was it something I said last night?" I searched his face in the semi-darkness. "Nate, what's going on? This is so sudden."

He let his hands hang by his side. "I agree. It probably does seem sudden, looking from the outside. But, I knew this day would come. The day I was willing to leave Carver, my dream job, for ... for someone special."

"Nate, you're not making a lick of sense."

He chuckled as he gazed out over the shifting silhouettes of dancing students. "You're starting to sound like a real Southern girl now."

"What's going on? Please —"

"I'm falling in love with you, Dr. Katrina Mason."

My heart skipped a beat.

He loves me.

"From the moment I said your name in the interview and shook your hand, I knew from that moment. When I started this job, I told God that He would have to send my woman through church because if He sent her through school then I'd have to leave."

"Why? Why do you have to leave?"

"The school district has a policy against fraternization."

"You ... you don't know me that well. Last night, you told me about your skeletons. I've got mine too."

"I know."

"How?" My mind went to Ernie Goode, and my face grew hot with embarrassment. "How long have you known? Was it Ernie?"

"Ernie hinted at some stuff, but I didn't want to believe him. After I almost kissed you, I found a private investigation service online and paid for them to look Trina Mason up. I know that's kinda weird. Getting a PI to check up on a woman you're falling in love with."

I stood in shock. I wasn't sure where this was going.

"Nate, stop."

Nate went on. "I'll be honest, I've been attracted to female colleagues before. The bat of the eyes. The swish of the hips. It's alluring. The power I wield as their boss. It's tempting and scary all at the same time. But it was different with you. It was like God was telling me you were the one. The one worth giving up my dream for."

Tears tumbled down my cheeks. "Nate ..."

He took my hands in his. "No, let me finish. I didn't tell you everything last night. Since I know so much more about you, it's only fitting that I tell you the rest of my story. The woman who gave birth to my child also gave birth to Dion."

Letting me go, Nate paused and looked over to where Dion stood on the stage, announcing the next total.

"He has a different birth dad, of course. Dion was four years old when I got involved with his mother. I didn't know she was leaving him in their apartment alone to be with me. He's my Ebenezer. My stone of help. With his crazy self. I thank God for him every single day."

Grace.

"Katrina, you're not a super woman and I sure ain't no superman, but I think He meant for us to meet. Are you willing to give me a chance?"

My heart hammered in my chest. My mouth was dry. My mind went blank and awhirl at once.

"You have bewitched me heart and soul, Katrina. And I never want to be away from you, but I have to leave Carver if there is to be a future for us. Say something please."

My lips moved but no words came out. I had no idea he had been thinking these things.

He hung his head. "I'm stupid. I've come on too strong and said too much."

"No, no. Please don't say that." I touched his hand.

His long, warm fingers wrapped around mine. I felt giddy and naughty at the same time, like a kid at a school dance holding a guy's hand for the first time. But this wasn't just any guy. This was the man I had dreamed about being with... for weeks.

"Nate," I said.

He looked into my eyes and I turned to mush. "Dance with me please."

Grinning, he pulled me to his side as the first strains of the next song started. As if by magic, a path to the dance floor cleared. The students shifted as we came to stand in the center under the disco ball 'moon'.

The words of Billie Holiday's *Blue Moon* filled the air. The room seemed to reverberate with the song as the students joined in.

"I love you, Nate Thomas," I said and rested my cheek against his lapel. The warmth seeping through the wool fabric was soothing against my skin.

It felt good to tell him how I truly felt. "Did you hear me, Nate?"

The rumble of his laugh shook my body. "Oh yeah, I heard you."

I craned my neck to look into his eyes. A soft glow from the spotlight above the moon bathed his bold features in golden light.

"Look," he said. "We're dancing on golden moonbeams."

"I kind of like dancing on the moon."

He gave me a soft peck on the lips. "Me too, Dr. Katrina. Me too."

I pulled his head closer and we lengthened the kiss.

"Hey, Mr. Thomas," one of the students yelled. "I thought you said there wouldn't be no kissing on the moon."

We broke the kiss and laughed. "These kids are all yours now, Dr. Katrina."

Mr. and Mrs. Warren waltzed by, putting down moves like they were on *Dancing with the Stars*.

"They're not kissing, young man," Mr. Warren said. "They are hugging. Kids these days don't know nothing."

About the Author

Linda Leigh Hargrove has been writing stories since high school. She's an engineer, a multi-published fiction author, a mother of three boys, and a wife of more than 25 years. Linda is a North Carolina native and tinkers on 3D printers in her free time. Her life motto, "She is no fool who gives what she cannot keep to gain what she cannot lose", governs every business decision. Find out more about her work at LLHargrove.com.

Love Called My Name
Alicia Fleming

The rain pounded against the window while Sierra sat in her car crying, looking at the lake, listening to the sound of the rain. *I call your name* by Switch played in the background. She thought her heart would burst at any moment, all Sierra could do was cry.

"God, how did I go from being happily married to a widow in the matter of a few years? My life was perfect. I had a great husband, a beautiful home in the country... Now, my home is just a big empty house."

It was the anniversary of her husband's death, and Sierra reminisced about their times with family and friends, wonderful vacations. They had created beautiful memories in their short time together. Her mind drifted back to the first time they met.

Sierra was headed on home summer break, but a spring storm had grounded flights at Patrick Henry airport. Several people waited in line to have their flights reassigned, Sierra along with them. Out the corner of her eye, the athletic build of a guy caught her attention. He was tall, about 6'3", long legs and built like a pro basketball player. She liked what she saw.

Trying to take him in without appearing desperate, she called her mom to let her know the flight was delayed. The guy finished at the counter and walked slowly past her, making eye contact. He smiled and mouthed hello. Yea, she definitely liked what she saw.

Sierra got her flight changed and sat down to read. She had a long wait before the next plane back to her hometown so she decided to read a book she had with her. A deep Barry White sounding voice interrupted her reading. "Excuse me, is this seat taken?"

Sierra looked up. It was the handsome guy from earlier. She stared into his light brown eyes that complemented his caramel brown complexion. A gorgeous set of pearly, white teeth were arched into a smile. She felt butterflies in her stomach. She had always been a sucker for a beautiful smile and pretty eyes. She wanted to melt into her seat in more ways than one.

"No, no one is sitting here."

"Thanks," he smiled. "I'm Harper, by the way. And you are?"

"I'm sorry. Um, I'm Sierra."

"Lovely name for a lovely lady."

"Thank you," Sierra blushed.

"Sierra," he repeated her name with his thick New York accent.

Sierra felt all doughy inside — warm and gooey, like hot caramel poured over a perfectly rounded scoop of ice cream. *Here goes that feeling again.* Sierra hadn't ever experienced these feelings this guy evoked in her, and she wasn't sure what it all meant.

"Yes."

"Where are you headed to?"

"I'm headed back home to Nashville. What about you?"

"Headed back home as well. I'm originally from New York, but I live in Los Angeles now. I love the weather in California. Couldn't take the winters in New York another year, so I moved out to LA with a couple of friends and I've been there ever since."

"What about your family? What did they have to say about you moving?"

A tense, awkward silence settled between them.

Watching his Adam's apple bob as he swallowed, Sierra rushed to fill the space. "I'm sorry. I didn't mean to be intrusive."

His easy smile disappeared. "No, no problem. It's just... My parents are both deceased."

She touched his arms. "Ohhh. I'm so sorry. I..."

"No, don't be, you had no way of knowing." Harper shook his head. "So, Sierra, tell me about yourself."

"Well, there's not much to tell. I'm from Nashville, Tennessee, so I'm a true country girl."

"Yea, a black country girl. I've never heard of such."

"Well, you have now."

They both laughed.

"I grew up in a suburb about twenty minutes outside of Nashville, and my family is into farming along with working for one of the big manufacturers in the area. I grew up with cows and horses, and of course a garden."

"Get out of here, you are country," Harper exclaimed.

Sierra mimicked him, but she did a horrible job of trying to imitate his New York accent.

"Hey, do me a favor and don't ever try that when you are in New York," Harper laughed.

The minutes passed into hours as they bantered back and forth until Sierra heard the attendant call for her flight to begin pre-boarding.

"Well, Harper, it's been nice chatting with you. But it's time for me to go."

"Man, the time went by too fast. I hope you have a safe flight. But listen, you think it might be okay if I get those digits before you take off?"

"Oh really? Well, Mr. New York, I guess you can do that if you smile for me and say please."

Harper obliged, and she gave him her number.

"I hope to talk to you soon. By the way, where do you go to college?"

"How did you know I was in college?"

"Duh." He pointed to her baseball cap that held her ponytail. Sierra had forgotten that she had on one of her sorority hats.

"I go to Hampton," Sierra said.

"Get out of here. So, do I. Why haven't I seen you around campus?"

"I kind of stay to myself. I'm somewhat of an introvert. I get out every now and then, but not a lot."

"Hmmmm. Well, I really enjoyed chatting with you, Sierra, and I hope to talk to you soon or better yet, see you around campus."

They said their goodbyes, and Sierra wondered whether or not she would hear from Harper again. She hadn't had much experience dating and wasn't really looking for things to change. Her mind was set on finishing school and starting her career. She didn't want all the drama that came along with dating.

A few weeks after returning to campus for the fall semester, Sierra heard someone call her name. She realized it was Harper.

"Sierra, I've been looking all over campus for you."

Sierra felt the same fluttering that she felt when Harper introduced himself at the airport. Her palms became sweaty, and she felt her body temperature rising.

Why is this guy having this kind of effect on me? Geez, I must be tripping.

He rushed toward her. "Can I walk you to your next class?"

"Well, sure, if you want to. It's such a beautiful day. I hate I have to go to class."

"Then don't."

"What? I can't be skipping class."

"You can if you're going to lunch with me."

"Really now?"

"Really," He nodded. "I was just joking about you cutting class, but I would like to take you to lunch or dinner one day or night this week."

"Well, okay," Sierra said shyly.

"You weren't joking about being shy."

And so, their love story began. Sierra had never felt more comfortable being herself with anyone until Harper. After a whirlwind romance, they married six months after graduating from Hampton University.

The rain beat down on her window even harder. Sierra didn't think her heart would ever mend. She didn't understand how God had allowed her heart to hold so much love only to have it shattered. There were nights Sierra woke up screaming. Her subconscious replayed the police coming to their home to relay the bad news. She knew something was wrong when Harper hadn't arrived home at his usual time, but she tried not to panic. She had dozed off on the couch waiting for him when the doorbell rang. A state trooper stood at the door when Sierra answered. He said Harper had been killed in a car accident and everything else became a blur. Sierra spent what seemed like days in bed crying. She didn't think she would ever get through the next second or the next day. But she did – one day at a time.

The rain continued pounding against her window, and Sierra continued to let her mind drift, thinking of intimate moments she and Harper shared. The two of them acting silly with one another, wrestling on the floor, just having fun being with one another. Sierra wasn't sure if she would ever find love again or if she even wanted to. Rain thrashed against her window reminding her of the way death had beat away her life with Harper.

Five Years Later

Sierra still felt beat down by death. She missed Harper, and while she had managed to go on with life, she went to grief counseling to work through the daily routine of life. She had met a really nice guy in her class who was also widowed. Handsome, tall like Harper with a beautiful smile, his name was Blaine, and he always made her laugh. It had been a long time since Sierra laughed, and this guy was hysterical. It's almost like he knew what she needed, but she couldn't even think about getting close to anyone or letting another man into her heart. She felt like she would be betraying Harper if she fell in love with someone else.

"Sierra, why you always looking so serious?" Blaine asked. "You know it takes less muscles to smile than to frown."

Sierra didn't always feel like smiling. That's why she kept to herself. She'd rather be alone with her thoughts of Harper. But one day, after a session, Blaine caught up with her before she could get away.

"Hey, Sierra, why don't you join the rest of us for lunch? We are going to the little café around the corner. Join us," he smiled. "I'm not taking no for an answer. You're always going off by yourself or sitting in your car on our breaks. You should hang out with the rest of us. It'll be fun."

"Okay, I guess I can do that." Sierra wasn't big on crowds, but she wanted to come out of her comfort zone and meet more people. Three or four different conversations were going on at the large table occupied by most of the class, and Blaine started chatting with Sierra.

"So, Sierra, what do you do for a living?"

"I'm a VP of Marketing for one of the major hotel chains in the area. I handle marketing and public relations for them."

"Wow, that sounds pretty interesting. You seem so quiet."

"Well, I enjoy my job. It has given me some great opportunities over the years."

"What about you?"

"I work for American Airlines."

Impressive. "Really? What do you do?"

"I am a pilot so I'm here, there and everywhere like Superman."

They both laughed.

"What? Was that a smile and a laugh?"

"Stop! You act as if I don't ever smile or laugh."

"You don't, at least not a whole lot. When you first joined our class, I thought you were stuck up. You came in with your little business suit on and your designer briefcase looking all professional and just sat down, not talking with anyone.

"Well, I'm an introvert, Blaine, and the last couple of years have been really hard. But I am trying to get out of this funk and get back into life. That's why I said yes to your invitation." She thrummed her fingers on the table. "It's just hard, you know?"

He covered her fingers with his hand. She stopped thrumming and looked up. "Yea, Sierra, I do know." He released her hand. "When my wife and daughter died, I thought my world had ended. There were days I really didn't want to go on without them, but I remember my mama and my grandma saying, 'Baby, just take it one day at a time, one hour at a time, one minute at a time and you will be alright. Trust in the Lord and keep your hand in His hand.'" Sierra could identify with the haunted look on Blaine's face. She would wager that losing his wife and child had been traumatic for him.

"What about you, Sierra? What brings you to this class?"

"My husband was killed in a car accident five years ago. It was all so unexpected and like I said, I want to move on with life, but I just haven't had the mindset to do so. I've basically spent the last few years working, going home and then going for a run or going to the gym. I think my friends got tired of always trying to cheer me up and they didn't know what else to do so I've kind of become a loner. But, I'm used to being alone. I do a lot of reading and watching television when I'm not traveling for work."

"Sounds like you need to change some of that and get back in the game of life."

"I agree, that's why I'm in this class. I'm hoping to learn some coping skills so I can keep moving forward."

"I think we have a few things in common, Ms. Sierra. Here's to the future, hopefully it will all be good."

Sierra started going to lunch with Blaine and the group on a regular basis. She enjoyed the conversations and started interacting more with others in the class, meeting up for coffee or going to the movies. After many hours of conversation, she and Blaine developed a familiar rapport with one another. He made her laugh, hysterically, every chance he got. He complimented her and told her she was beautiful, often making her blush. Sierra enjoyed being the center of his attention. She had missed that. One day another guy in the class tried to ask her out, and Blaine blocked him.

"Hmmmm, Blaine, how do you know I wasn't interested in going out with that guy?" Sierra asked him.

"Now, why would you be interested in going out with him and you have me right here at your disposal? If you go out with anybody, Ms. Sierra, it better be with me, your new best friend."

Sierra smiled sheepishly and laughed. "Well, Mr. Blaine, it sounds like you were a little bit jealous."

"I'm not jealous. I just know what I like, and I like you. I have a great time with you, Sierra. I would like the honor of taking you to dinner on Saturday night if that's okay with you."

Before Sierra realized it, she had agreed to have dinner with Blaine. She thought about it, but it was as if he read her mind.

"There's no changing your mind once you've given me your answer."

They made a date for the weekend and started dating consistently from that point on. They talked about their feelings and what it was like to lose someone so close to your heart. They shared their future dreams and aspirations and started working out together. Sierra could tell there was chemistry with Blaine, but she refused to let her guard down.

One night after a long run, Blaine asked if he could take a shower and put on some fresh clothes and Sierra agreed. As he took off his shirt, Sierra noticed his chiseled abs and muscular arms. She had already checked out his muscular legs on their run, but now she was seeing all of him in his glory and she liked what she saw. Sierra's body sprung to life with thoughts and feelings she hadn't had in some time, and she wasn't sure what to do with them. As she poured them both glasses of wine, Blaine exited the bathroom with a towel around his waist. Sierra hurried to turn away, but not before noticing Blaine's beautiful skin and the water droplets on his chest and back. Her mind went places it hadn't been since Harper. She sipped her wine and let her mind continue to wander while looking at Blaine's toned body.

"Oh. I'm sorry. I thought you were in the other room. I left my bag."

She shook her head. "No problem. Would you like a glass of wine?"

"Sure, I'll have some as soon as I get dressed."

Yes, Lawd, please let him put some clothes on.

Before she could take another sip, Blaine came towards her. "On second thought, I will have a sip." He looked at her and took a sip of wine, then leaned in close, lifting her chin. "I've been wanting to do this for some time." He gave her a tender, sweet kiss.

Sierra didn't open her eyes.

"Girl, are you okay?"

"Yes, I... I was...just not expecting that. But, it was a very nice surprise."

"Well then, if I'm not being too forward, I'd like to do it again." Blaine pulled her into him and kissed her passionately.

Sierra was literally swept away. Her body was feeling things it had not felt in years, and she was overwhelmed. She started crying, and Blaine stopped kissing her.

He stepped back. "Sierra, it's okay. We don't have to do anything you aren't ready to do. Understand me?"

Sierra shook her head. "I'm sorry, I don't know if I'm ready for all this. I do have feelings for you, Blaine, and I thought I was ready. But, I don't think I am."

"We are both vulnerable, Sierra. Having a rollercoaster of emotions isn't abnormal. We can take things as slow as you want. I don't want to do anything that will damage either of us emotionally. We've been through enough. Why don't you go take a shower? I'll put on my clothes and fix dinner for us. "

Sierra smiled and went into her bedroom to take a shower. When she returned, Blaine was fully clothed with dinner preparations underway. After their meal, they spent rest of the evening talking and kissing, but it never went any further. She appreciated Blaine's willingness to wait on her.

Sierra and Blaine did everything together. While some things were familiar activities she had done with Harper, Blaine introduced her to all kinds of new stuff as well. They started practicing martial arts, yoga, and riding bikes together. With Blaine's flight schedule, they weren't together all the time, but life had taught them both to make the most of every moment.

Sierra remembered the first time they made love. It was everything she thought it would be and more. They couldn't get enough of each other, and for the first time in years, Sierra opened her heart to another man. She was on cloud nine, and then the rainstorm came. Blaine took her to a small romantic restaurant, and she could tell something was on his mind.

"Babe, you okay?"

"Yes and no," Blaine said. "But let's get through dinner and then we'll talk about it. I just want to enjoy this night with you after being on the road for the last couple of weeks."

After dinner and dessert, Blaine grabbed her hand.

"Sierra, this past year has been amazing. I miss you when I'm gone, and I can't wait to get back here to see you. I love it when we're together. You bring out the best in me, and I hope I have been doing the same for you."

Sierra smiled. "But..."

"The airline has asked me to relocate from California to the east coast, Baltimore.

"Oh. So, what did you tell them?"

"I told them I needed to talk it over with my wife and get back to them."

"What?"

He smiled at her and pulled out a little black box.

Sierra gasped. "Blaine, what in the world?"

Blaine got down on one knee. "Sierra, will you marry me?"

Sierra had tears in her eyes. "Oh my God. Blaine, are you serious?"

"Serious as a heart attack, girl. I don't want to make a move without you."

"Blaine, this is so sudden. We haven't really talked about moving to the next step."

"I know. But I know, Sierra, that I want you in my life. And I want you to help me make this decision. For now, I'm getting up off of my knee because you're scaring me by not answering."

"I'm sorry. You just caught me off guard, Blaine. I really care about you and I love spending time with you, but I don't know if I'm ready to be your wife just yet." Sierra could see the hurt on Blaine's face, and she regretted not being as sure about them and their relationship.

"I had news to share with you as well. My company just offered me another position that would involve training other directors and vice presidents, and I wanted to talk to you about it as well. Crazy, right? Both of us with good news regarding our careers." She looked at the ring and then at him. "Blaine, this ring is fabulous, and I so want to put it on, but I need some time to think about this."

"I'll give you all the time you need, Sierra, but boy am I glad I didn't do this in front of a lot of people." He shook his head. "You just broke a brother's face big time."

"I'm sorry, babe."

"No, no. I should have put out some feelers with you, but I was trying to be spontaneous." Blaine laughed. "Note to self, don't do that again,"

"Please, keep the ring. Try it on, whatever, but promise me you'll give me an answer soon. I have to let the airlines know something by the end of next week, but I may be able to extend it out a few weeks."

They finished their dinner and continued talking. Sierra even put on the engagement ring which made

Blaine smile. She loved seeing his big smile, but as much as Sierra was into Blaine, she just didn't know if she was ready. She had loved being married and loved the idea of marriage, but she almost felt like she needed to take an adventure by herself before she decided to make another lifetime commitment. Over the years, she had learned that life was hard, and she didn't know if she could handle another hard blow.

"Sierra, earth calling Sierra," Blaine said. "Care to tell me why you just left me for a few minutes."

"I'm sorry. I was just caught up in my thoughts."

"Sierra, I know this is hard for you. It's hard for me. Neither one of us will ever forget what we had with our first spouse. But at some point, we have to move on with life. I'm ready to do that, and I hope you are as well. But, I don't want to pressure you if you're not ready. That's how much I love you, woman, I'm willing to wait until you're ready."

Sierra smiled at Blaine and planted a big kiss on him. "Well, on that note, I say we get out of here."

"Check please," Blaine called out, and they both laughed.

Three Weeks Later

"Sierra. Hey, babe, why don't you come over tonight? Let me cook dinner for you." Sierra knew it was time to give Blaine an answer. She had been dodging him over the last week because she hadn't made up her mind. With Blaine taking this job, Sierra would have to move halfway across the country and start a new life, and she was still having doubts.

"Okay, what time should I come over?"

"Let's say 7:30."

"Okay, I'll see you then."

"Sierra, you know I love you right?"

"I do, Blaine and I love you too." They hung up the phone. Lord, what am I going to do? I am going to have to give this man an answer about marrying him and starting a new life.

Sierra was running out of excuses. He had already told her she wouldn't have to work unless she wanted to, they would be fine financially. She could start her own business or stay home and do nothing, alluding to the fact that he would love to start a family.

After Harper died, Sierra hadn't thought about any of these things anymore. She had been so set on doing them with Harper. Now, reality had set in that she could still do them with someone else, but it almost felt like she was cheating on Harper. Sierra went to the cemetery and sat at Harper's grave.

"Harper, I know it's been a while since I've been out here and I'm sorry. I met a really nice guy name Blaine and to make a long story short, I think I love him, but I feel guilty loving him because I will always love you. He wants me to marry him and move thousands of miles away, and I just don't know if I'm ready to do that yet. I have compared him to you. I have studied his ways and mannerisms, and he's not you but he's a really great guy. I miss you so much, Harper, and there are days that I still think about you. I know you're probably saying, then what's the problem? I'm scared, Harper. What if I'm always comparing him to you or what if we get married and I have problems adjusting. What if it's too soon? You have been gone from me for more than five years now, but there are days when it seems like everything just happened yesterday. I don't know if I can give my all to Blaine when part of my heart still belongs to you." Sierra had learned things about herself in grief counseling, but she still felt like there were things she didn't know about herself. Was she really over Harper and ready to move on?

Later That Night

Sierra had been a chatterbox through the delicious grilled steaks, salmon, wild rice, asparagus and salad that Blaine had prepared. But the homemade cheesecake with strawberries on top for dessert rendered her mute.

"Wow, Blaine, you fixed a gourmet meal tonight. And it was... You know, it was just okay."

He gave her an incredulous look. "It was just okay?"

She hugged him and laughed. "It was deliciously divine, babe."

"Well, I will take that as a compliment. Deliciously divine just like you."

Sierra blushed. "Boy, bye. I'll do the dishes since you cooked this amazing dinner. You must have thought I was famished with as much food as you fixed."

"No, I just wanted to make sure there was enough for you to take for lunch the next day." *See, it's the little things like this. He is so doggone thoughtful.*

"Woman, I'll help clean the kitchen. As pastor says, 'many hands make for light work.'"

"Trust me, I don't mind you being in the kitchen, so you can help. But will that continue is the question?"

"Well, my mama and daddy taught me not to start something you weren't going to keep doing."

"I will amen that," Sierra said.

"You know that works both ways, right?" Blaine smiled at Sierra.

They both laughed. She loved the way he made her laugh.

"Let me pour us a glass of wine and we can sit down and talk."

Here we go. Sierra said to herself.

"So, have you given any more thought to my proposal and moving with me?"

"I have. And after careful consideration, I have put together a list of my requirements and demands." Sierra whipped out a long piece of paper that looked like Santa's Christmas list. She could barely contain herself.

Blaine had the funniest, confused look on his face. "What in the world?"

Sierra started laughing. She either talked too much or laughed too much when she got nervous. "Boy, I'm just playing with you. Seriously though, I have given it a lot of thought, and I would love to become Mrs. Blaine Johnson."

Blaine whisked Sierra off her feet and twirled her around the room, smiling and hugging her.

"Oh my God, we have so much to do. I have to let them know at work. You have to turn in your notice at your job. We have two houses to pack up and then we need to look for a new place to live, plan a wedding..."

Sierra could feel the excitement leaving her. As Blaine continued smiling and naming off things to do, she started to feel sick to her stomach.

The plan was for Blaine to move to the East Coast a couple of weeks ahead of her to get everything set up at their new place. Then they would focus on the wedding. Sierra wanted a small intimate ceremony, but Blaine wanted a big wedding with all of their family and friends. They had so much to do, Sierra couldn't keep up with everything, and she was internalizing all of her anxiety. Sierra was trapped in her own thoughts, none of which she shared with Blaine. He commented that she seemed distant, but she shrugged it off as having too much to do. To be honest, she was having second thoughts about everything, but she didn't know how to tell Blaine. Overwhelmed by all the sudden changes, she was hiding her anxiety attacks from him and having a hard time sleeping. Finally, the day came for Blaine to leave. Sierra drove him to the airport.

"Here you go, babe," She handed him a gift. "It's just a little something but promise me you won't open it until you get to the new place."

"Aren't you sweet?"

Sierra offered him a slight smile. She leaned into his body absorbing the smell of his cologne, feeling his muscles against her body. She gave him a kiss and a big hug. "Blaine, I do love you. I want you to remember that."

"Well sure, babe, I know that. But don't look so sad, we'll see each other in a few days."

"Yea, we will." She stepped back. "Well, you better get going so you won't miss your flight."

"I'll call you after I land."

Sierra nodded. She gave him a passionate kiss and waved goodbye.

"Hmm, something felt off about that," Blaine said as he headed toward the gate. "I think all of the changes has Sierra tripping and now I'm tripping."

When he landed, Blaine had gotten sidetracked with a fellow pilot and forgot to call Sierra. "I'll call her after I shower and open my gift." Blaine headed to their new place and let the jets of the rain shower wash the stress of the day away. Refreshed, he put on his pajamas and poured himself a glass of wine.

"Now, let me open up this surprise my baby got for me." Blaine opened the gift box, and there was an envelope inside. He unfolded it.

Dear Blaine,

I don't even know where to start but I just want to start off by letting you know that you have been one of the best things that ever happened to me. My life was empty before I met you and I was still dealing with my grief and everything that happened to me. Life didn't seem fair and there were days that I just wanted to give up and die and then I met you in class.

Blaine smiled to himself, thinking about how grateful he was to have a second chance at love. He continued reading.

When I first started talking to you, I had this feeling in the pit of my stomach that I still can't explain. It was butterflies and adrenaline all mixed together. Trust me, I never thought I would fall in love again. Harper was my one true love and I didn't know how to handle being with anyone else. You are an awesome man, and I am blessed to call you my fiancé. Any woman would be happy to have you as their man. And you being such a great guy makes it all the harder for me to say what I'm about to say.

All kinds of thoughts ran through his head. Was she unhappy? Was she pregnant? What was she trying to say?

Blaine, I will not be joining you in Baltimore, and I cannot marry you at the present time. All of the planning and preparation over the last month has stressed me out. I feel like I am suffocating right now, and I just need some air and some time and space. Please do not try to reach me.

Tears welled up in his eyes. "I knew in my spirit something wasn't right at the airport."

I have quit my job and by the time you read this, I will be on a flight out of the country.

"No, Sierra, no. Please don't do this to us," Blaine yelled at the letter.

My cell phone will be disconnected until I decide to return. I am so sorry to do this to you this way, but I just couldn't tell you face to face that I wasn't ready. You deserve someone who is ready to move on and let go of their past. I am just not ready to completely let go of Harper and what I had with him. I have left the engagement ring in the top drawer in your bedroom at your house. I don't feel right keeping it if we're not getting married. I pray you will find it in your heart to forgive me, but I just need some time alone. Sincerely and with all my love, Sierra.

Blaine dropped the letter and fell across the bed sobbing. His heart had just been ripped out and, like with the death of his wife and child, he didn't even see it coming. It was totally unexpected just like the last time.

Almost at the same time that Blaine was reading his letter, Sierra was looking out the window of a plane into the darkness with tears rolling down her face wondering if she had just made the biggest mistake of her life.

Two Years Later

After that letter, Sierra figured she would probably never see or hear from Blaine again. She regretted how she handled things but being away the last couple of years had helped her find herself and figure out what she wanted to do with the rest of her life. She had developed a passion for photography and capturing priceless moments in time as she called them. After interning with a skilled and highly sought-after photographer in South Africa, Sierra decided corporate America was no longer for her. She'd had her fill of all the greed and favoritism so she put in her notice, put her house on the market and cashed out her 401K to make a new start.

She thought often about Blaine and missed him terribly. She kept wondering if she should try and reach out to him, but every time she got up the nerve do it, she would hang up the phone before the call went through.

Her best friend, Terri Lynn kept insisting that time healed all wounds and that he probably understood what she was going through, but Sierra wasn't convinced.

"What if he isn't okay with how I handled things?" She asked Terri Lynn.

"Well, you won't know if you don't talk to him. I told you all along, you should have told him how you were feeling. But, what's done is done. You can't change it."

Sierra missed spending time with Blaine. She knew she was at a better place mentally, physically and spiritually. She was a lot more confident and sure of herself. The time away had been good for her. Still, she missed Blaine.

Sierra received a letter from National Geographic. They were interested in hosting a photography exhibit for her in Los Angeles and wanted to use some of her photos for a project they were working on. Sierra was so excited. She wanted to call Blaine and share the good news but then remembered she'd given up that right with her *Dear Blaine* letter.

She asked Terri Lynn to join her and made preparations for the exhibit. As Terri Lynn helped Sierra prepare for the exhibit, they laughed and cut up. In a more serious moment, Sierra confessed to Terri Lynn that she felt she had made a mistake by not marrying Blaine and she regretted her decision. But at the end of the day, she couldn't undo the pain she had caused him with the way she handled things.

National Geographic booked their first-class tickets to LA on American Airlines. *How ironic.* Sierra shook her head in disbelief.

"Isn't this crazy, girl? We end up getting booked on the same airline Blaine works for."

Her best friend laughed. "Only in Sierra's world would this happen."

"Now, all I need is for Blaine to be flying this plane," Sierra said.

"Girl, you never know what God is up to. You and Blaine could still end up together. Remember, God's ways are not our ways and His thoughts are not our thoughts." Terri Lynn smiled.

The exhibit was a big success, people called her a natural. Others said she was a gifted photographer. Several people placed orders for her photos, and National Geographic hinted at the possibility of offering her a freelance position with them.

"Terri Lynn, freelance work would be the best of both worlds. I could still have control over my work life and personal life. Not that I really have a personal life anymore."

Sierra and Terri Lynn wrapped up, and Sierra overheard Terri Lynn talking to someone whose voice sounded familiar. She shook her head. "That girl knows everybody. Here we are in LA and she knows somebody."

"Sierra, I'll be back in a minute," Terri Lynn yelled. Sierra turned to reply and couldn't believe her eyes.

"Sierra, how are you?"

The photos she held in hand floated to the ground and Sierra stopped dead in her tracks like she had seen a ghost. "Oh my God, Blaine!" She wasn't sure whether to hug him or extend her hand, but he reached out and hugged her.

"Blaine, I am so—"

He shook his head. "There's no need to apologize, Sierra. I get it. I was all caught up in my feelings at first, but then I realized the pressure. We were moving really fast. Yes, it hurt that you handled things the way you did, but I knew you needed the space. I was probably the one smothering you and rushing you into something you weren't ready for."

"Blaine, I have wanted to reach out to you so many times, but I always chickened out. Can you ever forgive me?"

"Yes, Sierra, I forgive you. I forgave you a long time ago."

Sierra could see Terri Lynn out the corner of her eye, not acting at all surprised.

"Did you know about this, Terri Lynn?"

"Who me?" Terri Lynn pointed at herself. "What you talking about?" She feigned innocence and waved her hand across the air. "Girl, bye."

Blaine started laughing.

"Well, what are you two going to do?" Terri Lynn moved toward them. "Keep wasting the precious time God has given you and miss out on love again. Both of you are working my last nerve. All kinds of lonely folks out here in the world and you two just keep running from one another." She turned to Blaine. "Blaine, do you still love Sierra?"

"Yes, I still love her. If only she understood how much, then she would have trusted me to give her all the space and time she needed."

"Sierra, do you still love Blaine?" Terri Lynn asked.

With tears in her eyes, Sierra nodded her head.

Blaine got down on one knee. "Sierra, would you do the honor of marrying me?"

She shrieked. "Yes, of course. If you'll still have me."

Like before, Blaine swept Sierra off her feet and spun her around. "Girl, I have been waiting on you. Terri Lynn has kept me abreast of all you were doing and making sure I knew you were okay."

The stare Sierra gave Terri Lynn made her shudder. "What? What was a BFF supposed to do in this situation? I didn't want the two of you to miss out on what God has for the both of you together."

They hugged Terri Lynn and Blaine said, "Excuse me for a second." He turned to Sierra and kissed her passionately.

"Now are you sure you want to be Mrs. Blaine Johnson?"

Sierra nodded. "I do."

The Next Year

Sierra looked down at the beautiful little boy and girl she had just delivered. She couldn't believe that she had gotten married and brought life into the world.

Blaine was beaming with pride. "Sierra, I'm so proud of you. You did a great job. Look at what we did together. I am so grateful God gave us an opportunity to get back together."

"Blaine Johnson, I am so happy that you gave me another opportunity to love you and give you these two beautiful babies. And, I am forever thankful that love called my name once again. I am blessed beyond measure." Sierra reached over and squeezed Blaine's hand. "Our new life together is amazing. God has given us both double for our heartache and trouble."

About the Author

Alicia has always had a passion for reading and writing. Growing up in Mt. Juliet, Tennessee – a suburb twenty minutes outside of Nashville, Alicia has always enjoyed the solitude that comes with reading and writing. Alicia graduated from Middle Tennessee State University (MTSU) years ago with a Bachelor of Science degree in Public Relations and realized her passion for writing. She wants to make an impact on people through her writing, travels and photography and desires that her gift be used to bless and encourage others in a positive way. When she is not spending time with her husband, David and adult daughter, Megan, Alicia enjoys reading, writing, traveling and just having fun with family and friends.

For the Love of You
Yolanda Johnson-Bryant

"Cabo San Lucas?" Serena's mother, Betty screamed. "This man is so full of surprises."

Serena was in awe herself. She had met the man of her dreams. He had wined and dined her and never once asked her to give up her virtue. She was sure their upcoming trip to a popular tourist destination would lead to a wedding proposal.

When Serena first met Gerard Nelson, she thought he was way out of her league. It's not that she didn't think highly of herself, she just assumed he was joking or trying to sow his wild oats when he initially pursued her. There were countless excuses with every no until she finally said yes. If anything had impressed her, it was his persistence. Nearly four months passed before Serena decided to meet Gerard for a cup of coffee. And another two months went by before she said yes to a lunch date and nine months before she agreed to dinner.

"When do you leave?" her mom asked.

"Next weekend."

Betty twitched her nose. "I sure hope you scheduled a wax for this week. Because if I had to judge by the hair on your legs, everywhere else is a jungle. If you know what I mean," she winked.

"Mother!" Serena didn't know why she was so surprised. This was her mother. She always said what she meant, meant what she said and never sugar coated anything. When God was handing out filters and couth, her mom had stepped out of line.

"Girl, bye. How do you think you got here? Wasn't no immaculate conception going on here. Immaculate ingestion maybe, but no immaculate conception."

If she could, Serena would have blushed. But her deep brown skin wouldn't allow her embarrassment to show. "As a matter of fact, I have a complete spa treatment scheduled this week. And, I'll be getting my hair and nails done."

"That's my girl," her mother said. "So, you think he's going to propose, huh?"

"I think so, but I'm not completely sure. I just feel it though."

"Well, I hope you're right. But if you're not, don't be discouraged. Remember, Jacob waited a very long time to get Rachel. Even after her sister tricked him, he wanted Rachel. And that's real love. If he wants you bad enough, he'll get you. But, it will all be done in God's timing."

"I know you're right. I'll go with no expectations except to enjoy time with my soulmate."

Betty looked at her daughter and shook her head. "Soulmate, schmolemate. Don't you mean, whomever God has put together, let no man..."

"We just came from church, I don't need another sermon."

Betty frowned, holding her hands up in defeat.

It was their Sunday ritual to go to church dressed to the nines, complete with hats, gloves, to-die-for shoes, and what they called, 'First Lady Suits'. After church, they would retreat to Serena's loft apartment in North Dallas, change clothes, still dressed to the nines, but less first ladyish, and head out for lunch. After lunch, the two ladies would go their separate ways, take a nap and then reconvene back at her parent's house. This had been the tradition in the Collin's household for decades.

The last few years had been especially hard for Serena, her mother, and her siblings. Their father had passed away three years prior from lung cancer. Mr. Collins owned a construction company and could often be seen working side by side with his workers. The doctor said ingesting the dust, chemicals, mold and asbestos from various job sites was more than likely the culprit for her father's demise. Mr. Collins had left his wife and two daughters a hefty inheritance and the family business to his two sons.

Serena and her mother arrived at Baby Does Restaurant at 12:30. As they were being seated, Serena's older sister, Terrie walked in. Serena waved and motioned to her sister.

"Great sermon today." Terrie approached Serena and their mother, hugging them both.

"Yes, it was," their mother said. "And right on time."

The waiter brought over mimosas and glasses of water.

In keeping with their Sunday tradition, they clinked their champagne flutes and said in unison, "To the Collins' ladies!"

"I didn't see my grandson and son-in-law in church today? Are Tyler and Bruce okay?" Betty asked Terrie.

"They were there. They were working on a project for the pastor for their upcoming Men's Day," she answered.

"Oh okay, I bet Tyler loves that."

Terrie nodded, "He won't stop talking about it."

The ladies made their way around the brunch buffet and returned to their table.

Well into their meal, Betty looked at Serena. "Should I tell her or are you?"

"Tell me what?" Terrie asked.

A moment of silence passed as Serena and her mom engaged in a staring match.

Betty huffed. "Your sister is going to Cabo with Gerard this weekend, and they may come back engaged."

Serena shook her head. "Can't take you nowhere," she said to her mother.

"Is it true, sis?" Terrie asked.

"I don't know for sure, but my gut says it could happen."

"I sure hope so." Terrie reached across the table and squeezed her sister's hand. "I'm so happy for you, Serena. I've always wanted you to share the kind of love Bruce and I have, two beautiful children, living our dreams. You deserve to be blessed like that too."

"Thank you, sissy. That means a lot to me. We'll see what the future holds. I'm optimistic and cautious, but definitely open to every blessing God has in store for me," Serena said.

The ladies finished their meals, said their goodbyes and promised to see each other later at the family house.

* * *

Serena took off work early. She had already packed for her trip, but she wanted to make sure she had everything in order before Gerard picked her up. She unpacked and repacked, carefully inspecting each piece of clothing. She switched the Dolce and Gabbana Light Blue fragrance for Unforgiveable and ran a clear coat of polish over her nails before ensuring all her makeup and hair care products were tucked away in their special compartment. A natural beauty with flawless dark skin, Serena didn't require a lot of makeup. She wore eyeliner, mascara and lipstick with a little concealer and bronzer to hide the faint circles under her eyes and a small scar along the side of her chin, courtesy of the family cat.

She locked her valuables in her hidden safe and checked her security app to make sure signals transmitted from her security cameras. A text message came through while she was selecting a hat to wear to the tropical paradise. The ring tone told her it was Gerard. He had a thing about ringing the doorbell and so did Serena. There had been a rash of burglaries, rapes and assaults around the country. Men would ring the doorbells of poor suspecting citizens and before they knew it, it was too late. Serena's motto was, if one didn't call, one was not getting in. And if one stayed by the door too long, she would then alert the authorities. Everyone she knew, Gerard, her family and her friends knew of her rule.

She opened the door for Gerard. They embraced, and he kissed her on the forehead.

"Where's your luggage?" He looked over Serena's shoulder.

Serena turned and pointed. "Right there."

"That's it?"

"Yes, that's it."

"Just when I think you can't give me another reason to be in love with you, you go and do this."

"What?" Serena asked, dumbfounded.

"One small suitcase, a carryon and your purse? Do you know how many suitcases most women take on trips? They have to have three large suitcases, a large carryon, a backpack and their humungous purses."

"I'm not most women. Now, am I?"

Gerard shook his head. "I love your hair. New hair color?"

Serena loved that Gerard never missed an opportunity to compliment her or tell her how much she meant to him.

This wasn't Serena's first rodeo. In her thirty-five years, she had dated men from all walks of life, but the common thread from most of those relationships was she was always the giver and they were always the receiver. Reciprocity hadn't been something she was used to.

"I'm glad you like it," Serena said, twirling to give Gerard a fashion preview.

She set the security alarms and the two were off to the airport for their romantic weekend in beautiful Cabo.

* * *

"Honey, we're here." Gerard shook Serena's shoulder.

"I'm sorry, I fell asleep."

"No, no. It's okay. I want you to be rested for our eventful weekend. Besides, I think I dozed for about an hour or so myself."

When they arrived at the Pueblo Bonito Pacifica Resort, Serena's sixth sense was even stronger. She was seventy-five percent sure Gerard was going to pop the question. Out of the nice resorts and hotels he could have booked, Pueblo Bonito was royal status. The rooms started at four-hundred-dollars a night. And even though Serena knew Gerard could afford this kind of resort with his position as an options trader and financial advisor, none of their trips had ever been this extravagant.

When the bellhop led them to their room, Serena's eyes filled with awe. A sliding glass door led to an exquisite balcony overlooking the Pacific Ocean. She had seen beautiful beaches before, but none like this. Her attention was diverted back to the bellhop who was opening the door to the adjacent room.

"What's that about?" Serena asked Gerard.

"This is your room, and that one is mine," he answered.

Serena felt a little deflated. She was sure they'd be in the same room, sharing the same bed.

"Why two rooms? At this rate, are you crazy?"

"Crazy in love with you," he smiled.

"You're so corny. But seriously, we're staying an entire week. You're going to pay one-thousand-dollars or more a night for two rooms? I can't let you do that. What's wrong with the one bed?" Serena and Gerard had shared the same bed plenty of times before and behaved themselves. Sure, there was a few close calls. But Gerard, being the gentleman, he was, respected Serena's desire to stay celibate until she married again.

"This is absolutely ridiculous. Gerard, I appreciate everything you've done and everything you do for me, but I cannot be the kind of woman who would allow this much waste. I would have been happy at a Super 8 Motel, just as long as it was near the beach."

"Okay, baby, I had no idea you'd be this upset, but I'm gonna need you to get your hands out of my wallet. I'm a big boy. I know what I can and cannot afford. I'm smart enough to know whether or not I can do what I do. I do consider myself to be a little intelligent, you know."

The bellhop looked back and forth between Serena and Gerard, patiently waiting for his tip.

"I wasn't implying that. I just don't want you to think I'm the kind of woman who thinks she needs all of this."

"I know what kind of woman you are, woman. Now, cállate," he demanded.

The bellhop chuckled.

Serena didn't speak Spanish. "What did he just say to me?" she asked the bellhop.

"Well, putting it nicely, ma'am, the mister has asked that you silence yourself."

She turned to Gerard. "You told me to shut up?"

Gerard looked at the bellhop as if to say, "You know you don't break the man code, bruh."

The bellhop dipped his head. "My apologies, sir. My name is Matias, by the way. Here is my card. I'm at your beck and call for your entire stay. Call me day or night, anytime."

"Thank you, Matias," Gerard said, tipping Matias before he disappeared on the other side of the door.

Serena glared at him. Gerard was a muscular, six-foot-three inches. Anyone who looked at him knew he worked out on a regular basis. His close-cut hair and mustache and beard complimented his face. She loved men with well-groomed facial hair. His eyeglasses added to his appeal. A tall glass of vanilla latte with just the right amount of chocolate. Here she was mad at this man, and she still couldn't help but notice how scrumptious he looked. She shook her head.

"Look, baby. I know you're not that kind of woman, but you should know what kind of man I am. I wouldn't spend this kind of money on any woman but you. I've never spent this kind of money on anyone else. And no, I'm not trying to buy you. You have to understand that men are stupid sometimes. Not saying I'm not intelligent. They're two different things. When we love someone, we want to give them everything they deserve and more. Unfortunately, some men use money, material things and sex to do that. That being said, this is a part of me you're going to have to accept if we are going to have a future together."

Serena looked down at the floor. It was a small pill for her to swallow, but she did want a future with this man.

"Look, I know you're independent and that is one of the many things I love about you. Hell, with your inheritance and your position as CFO at the Howard Hughes Corporation, I know your finances are compatible to mine. I just want to do things for the woman I love. Is that okay with you?"

"Yes, but why two rooms? One would have sufficed. We've slept in the same bed before. You could have even gotten one room with two beds."

Gerard gave her that 'you're not listening' look. Serena digressed.

"So, what else do you have planned for us? Judging by the rooms, I know it's going to be something spectacular."

"You'll just have to wait and see. Won't you?" He kissed her on the forehead, and they embraced while staring out at the beautiful ocean.

"Hey, I'm paying for this view. Why are we looking at it from in here?"

"You've got a point," Serena agreed.

They moved to the balcony, and Gerard stood behind Serena enfolding her in his embrace. Chin nestled on her shoulder, they took in the breathtaking view. A breeze lifted, and speckles of water brushed their faces.

"You have good taste," Serena said.

"I know. That's why I chose you." Gerard kissed her cheek.

Serena was even more certain this would be the weekend he proposed.

"We are having a couple's massage after dinner. Then I think we'll just spend some time together alone in one of the rooms. After that, I'm going to tuck you in and retreat to my room."

"You're talking about bedtime already? You can't hang, old man?"

Gerard was forty-five, ten years older than Serena, but no one could tell from his outward appearance.

He picked her up over his shoulder. "You're going to eat those words one day."

* * *

Three days had passed since Gerard and Serena arrived at the resort and they had been going nonstop, like the Energizer Bunny. They had enjoyed exotic cuisine, snorkeled, ziplined, rode ATVs on the beach, gone on horse rides and went dolphin and whale watching. Gerard loved introducing Serena to new experiences and watching her expressions. He could tell she was in hog heaven.

Tonight, Gerard had something special planned for his lady, and she had no idea. Matias and the staff at the resort had been extremely helpful in planning his little secret. While he and Serena were out on today's excursions, the staff would make sure the tub in Serena's room was filled with tons of bubbles and pink rose petals. They would surround the bathroom with candles, and queue a romantic playlist. A basket of fresh fruit would be placed nearby. He would entrust Matias to place the 3-carat oval, diamond engagement ring in one of the strawberries. He had instructed him to drizzle the special fruit with white chocolate so he knew exactly which strawberry had the ring in it. Gerard knew Serena would flip if she knew the platinum engagement ring had set him back thirty-three thousand dollars. But it was just a drop in the bucket to him. He made that much on one options trade. Technology stocks had made him rich, and he continued to build his wealth. Gerard knew Serena would find his spending habits haphazard and frivolous. He wouldn't tell her how much the ring cost, and he hoped she wouldn't ask. If she did, he'd lie until the cows came home.

Gerard knew he was taking a chance bathing with Serena in the same tub. If she chose to wear a bathing suit, he was okay with that, but this would be the day and the way he proposed. He wanted her, and he wanted her to be his wife. He finalized the plans with Matias and dressed for their day of adventure.

He heard a knock on the door that separated their rooms. "Are you decent?" Serena asked through the door.

"I am," he called out.

Gerard tucked his sleeveless muscle shirt into his shorts as Serena entered the room in a green floral bathing suit that crisscrossed at the shoulders with a pair of white linen shorts and brown sandals.

The suit enhanced her bosom. "Don't you look beautiful?"

"You don't look so bad yourself. But let one woman look at you and we're going to have a problem." She chuckled.

Gerard took Serena in his arms and kissed her—deeply, passionately.

She broke the kiss. "Be right back," she murmured.

Gerard nodded. He would bet a million dollars she had become aroused. His own body tingled as his nature rose. He prayed she did not feel it. He wanted that woman, and he wanted her bad. If he had to wait until they were married, they would have a short engagement.

Gerard took a piece of pineapple from the fresh fruit basket Matias had delivered earlier. His cell phone rang, but he ignored it. He knew it wasn't Serena because her specific ringtone was Pattie Labelle's *Love, Need and Want You*. Anyone else could leave a message. There would be no talk or thought of work during this trip. He waited to hear his phone beep indicating there was a message, but the beep never came. Instead, his phone rang again, and again, and again. Someone was desperately trying to reach him. The number had a 469-area code—Texas.

"Hello?"

"Ah, Gerard. Dr. Lang, here. I've been trying to reach you."

"Dr. Lang?"

"Yes, you know I wouldn't bother you while you're enjoying the beautiful waters of Cabo, but this is very important."

"How did you know I was in Cabo?"

"Well, you mentioned it to my nurse Janet. And Janet can't hold water."

Gerard laughed. "I see. So, to what do I owe this call?"

"We've received the results of your colonoscopy. We tested all three of the polyps that we found, and I'm afraid to say..." Dr. Lang became quiet.

"What is it, Doctor?" Gerard's heart was pounding, fast and strong, like it wanted to break through his chest.

Gerard turned as Serena walked into the room. She paused mid stride.

"What's wrong?" she mouthed.

Gerard stared at her, his expression blank.

"Gerard, one of the polyps tested positive for cancer. Are you sure you haven't experienced any symptoms, other than the ones you've already told me about?"

"Doctor, let me turn the radio down. I'm certain I didn't hear you clearly," Gerard said. Serena looked at him strangely. The only sounds coming into the room were the ocean's waves and faint chatter from guests sitting around the pool below. She took his arm and guided him to the couch.

"It's malignant, Gerard. You have cancer," Dr. Lang repeated the six-letter word no one ever wants to hear. "I'm just finding it hard to believe that you've not experienced any symptoms besides fatigue. I hate to say this, but I recommend you cut your vacation short. I'd like to get you in immediately for more tests. We may have a chance of defeating this, but it's imperative that we know exactly what we're working with."

Gerard felt like his entire life had been sucked out of his body. He started to sweat profusely, and the phone hit the floor.

Serena picked up his phone. "Baby, what is it?"

"I have cancer," Gerard said mechanically, looking straight ahead.

"Oh no, honey. Are they sure? You know those doctors don't know the same God we do. I'm sure this is some kind of mix-up."

Gerard knew the doctor spoke truth. He had been having symptoms but felt too manly to tell his doctor. For the last few months, he hadn't been able to stay out of the bathroom, urinating several times during the day, interrupting his sleep at night. His lower back and pelvic had been in excruciating pain, not to mention the blood he had found in his stool. He chocked it up to weightlifting and swore he would cut back.

"Cancer. Cancer. Cancer," Gerard repeated. His father had died of prostate cancer when he was a teenager.

"Baby, we are going to fight this. I'm here with you. I'll go through this with you. God is a miracle worker." Serena stood, pacing back and forth. Gerard watched as she worshipped and prayed, beseeching God to heal her soulmate and make him whole again.

"Yet, another one of the many things I love about you." He patted the cushion next to him, motioning for Serena to take a seat.

He intertwined their fingers. "This was supposed to be a special time."

"It has been. This is something I would have never done by myself. We've done more things in the last few days than others do in a lifetime."

"Yes, but when I say special, I mean..." He stopped and looked away. None of this was fair to Serena. He couldn't very well marry her now. She'd probably be a widow in a few short years. And there was a chance they wouldn't be able to have children. He'd be leaving her a grieving widow, but she had to know how deep his love for her went. He unzipped the backpack they had been using on their island adventures and pulled out the box that housed her engagement ring. Gerard took a deep breath.

"Tonight was going to be the night I asked you to be my wife." He opened the box and Serena's eyes grew wide.

"Oh. My. God," she said.

"And now—"

"And now what? You're not giving up, are you? We won't even know what's really going on until we get back home and you get more tests. The devil is a lie."

Gerard smiled at Serena. It just didn't seem fair that he would be missing out on a lifetime with the woman he loved. He wasn't giving up, but he was also a realist.

"No, I'm not giving up. It's just that—"

"Gerard, I've been waiting for this day all my life. Where is your faith, baby? God's got this."

"Serena Collins, will you do me the honor of being my wife?"

"You better believe it," Serena hugged Gerard. "I love you so much and we're going to beat this, together."

Gerard lifted her hand and placed the diamond on her ring finger.

"Just so you know, I'll wear this for now, but as soon as we get back home, you're returning the ring for a more modest one."

"You don't even know how much it cost. It wasn't much at all."

"Are we going to start this thing off with you lying to me? It's the same ring we looked at a while ago, and I told you there was no way I'd pay for a ring like that or wear a ring that cost that much."

Gerard wondered why he ever thought she wouldn't figure it out.

"Forty thousand? Really, Gerard?"

"I got a discount. It was only thirty-three."

She gave him the side-eye. "Do you see me laughing? I don't need to be scared every time I walk down the street wondering if someone is going to knock me over the head because they saw me with this expensive ring."

"I see your point. When we get back, I'll let you pick out the ring you want, even though you wanted that one."

"I didn't want this one. I just said it was beautiful, not that I wanted it."

Gerard didn't want to spend time bickering about something so trivial. If his days were numbered, he wanted to spend each one loving the woman of his dreams.

* * *

The doctor informed them Gerard had advanced stage four colon cancer and the cancer had already spread to other parts of his body. Gerard was told that he only had a few short weeks to live, and he decided he did not want to die alone. He married Serena days after returning from Cabo because he wanted to die knowing he had married the woman of his dreams.

Gerard surprised them all, living six more months before the disease overcame him. Serena took his death very hard, but she was with him every step of the way, just like she promised. The last words he said to her were, "Let love find you. Give love, receive love."

Serena swore she would never love another man, but Gerard told her he did not expect her to be unhappy in his absence. Serena was not trying to hear that. Even though their time had been cut short, God had truly blessed them both.

Gerard changed his will without Serena's knowledge, leaving her twenty-two million dollars. A millionaire in her own right, she opened a foundation in Gerard's name for cancer research with the money. She had lost her father to cancer and now her husband. She would make it her life's mission to find a cure for cancer.

* * *

"You know, baby, it's been a year since Gerard went to be with the Lord," her mother said during their Sunday brunch. "Don't you think it's time you start making yourself available again? I mean, you'll be forty in a couple of years. The older you get, the harder it will be to have children."

"Mama!" Her sister, Terrie scolded. "You need a filter, for real. Sometimes I wonder if you realize what comes out of your mouth."

"Lil' girl, I'm sixty-nine years old. If God ain't gave me a filter by now, he ain't neva' gon' give me one. So hush."

Terrie rolled her eyes at her mother. She knew her mother was right, but she also knew people grieved in their own way, however long it took. There was no set time on grief. She admired her sister. She had found the love of her life, lived a little, and he left her the world.

"Mother, I'm not interested in, as you say, getting back out there. I'm too busy. I don't have time for a man in my life right now with running the foundation and all." Serena had resigned from her position at the Howard Hughes Corporation and threw all she had into the foundation and cancer research, even going back to school for medical training. "Gerard was enough for me. I trust God's judgement. I would never want to betray my husband."

"Your husband is dead. I know that sounds bad, but it is reality. And if I knew anything about my son-in-law, I knew he lived in reality. You know I'm telling you the truth."

"Why are you trying to get me married off all of a sudden?" Serena asked.

"So you can give me more grandbabies."

"Terrie and Bruce gave you grandchildren. One each, a boy and a girl."

"I know, and I'm grateful. But Tyler and Kennedy need cousins to play with." Terrie cleared her throat. "Cousins with our blood. To help carry our legacy into the future."

"Mom, I know you're not being this persistent just because you want me to give you grandchildren."

Her mother was quiet for a moment.

Terrie looked from her mother to her sister. "Okay, here's the deal. Our mother wants you to remarry, not just for the sake of giving her more grandbabies. Ever since dad died, Mom has been lonely. She has a few regrets as a widow, and she doesn't want the same for you."

Serena watched as her mother teared up and excused herself from the table.

"I never knew." Serena shook her head.

"You were working. You were in love and then you were dealing with Gerard. You missed a few cues." Her sister shrugged her shoulders. "Every night before she says her prayers, Mama has an imaginary conversation with Dad."

"Maybe it's not imaginary. I believe spirits can comfort us, some even staying with us for a season. I know of a little girl whose brother was murdered by her mother's boyfriend. The little girl was sent to live with their grandmother and her brother's spirit followed them. The spirit stayed for about nine months until he was sure his sister was in good hands, and then he left. Mom could very well be talking to Dad."

"You're right, but I hate to see her feeling so lonely. She's trying to push you back into the dating scene, I wish she would get back out there herself. And for the record, I think you should too. I knew my brother-in-law well, and I know he would want you to find love again. He knows you'll never find a love that surpasses the one you and he had, but I know for a fact he wouldn't want you to be alone. He'd want you to love again."

"Hmm, and you know that for a fact? How is it that you know that for a fact?" Serena was tired of everyone trying to fix her when she wasn't broken.

Terrie bowed her head. "Gerard and I had a conversation shortly before he died. He told me to look after you and once you'd stopped grieving, to assure you that he'd want you to love again."

"He told you that?"

Terrie looked her sister in the eye and nodded. "Yes, he did."

"What else did he tell you?"

"Shortly before Gerard died, he called and said he wanted to see his niece and nephew. I took the kids to the hospital so they could spend some time with their uncle and say their goodbyes. Before we left, he shared his heart and concerns about you, and I promised I would do my best to carry out his wishes."

Terrie reached over and squeezed her sister's hand as tears fell from Serena's eyes.

"That was my Gerard, always taking care of me, making sure I had what I needed. And, all the more reason why there will never be another man that could live up to him. Gerard will always be my soulmate."

Terrie wrapped her arms around her sister. "Sissy, I didn't mean to make you cry, but that's what he wants for you."

"I didn't mean to make you cry. I wasn't trying to hurt you," her mom said walking up behind them.

"I know, Mom. I know."

"Terrie is right, I don't want you to be alone. I want you happy and sharing your life with someone, and I do want more grandbabies."

Serena looked from her mother to her sister, then closed her eyes. She pictured the day she and Gerard got married. When she opened her eyes, a chill spread throughout her body. She shivered a bit.

"Are you cold?" Her mom asked.

"No, I just had the strangest feeling."

"What? Are you okay?" Terrie inquired.

"Yes," she nodded. "It was just strange. So, what are the plans for Kennedy's birthday?" Serena asked, changing the subject.

"We're taking her and a group of friends to Great Wolf Lodge that weekend. Are you coming?"

"Unfortunately, not. That's the weekend of our missions trip to Africa."

"That's right. Are you prepared?"

"About as prepared as I can be."

"I don't know if I like you trekking off to Africa," her mom said. "I mean it's not like Africa is a two-hour plane ride away."

"Don't start doubting your faith now," Serena said. "God's got this. His will be done, right?"

"Amen," both Terrie and Betty said.

"Who all is going on this missions trip besides the pastor?" Her mom asked.

"A few of the deacons, Mrs. Mary, Mrs. Sara, Mr. Henry, Mr. Butler and a few of the teenagers."

"Greg isn't going?" Her mother asked, looking at Serena out the side of her eye.

"Who's Greg? You know our church is so big, I don't know half the people you guys know." Terrie said.

"Greg Pierce, Mary Pierce's son," Their mother said matter of factly.

"Well, what's the four-one-one on this Greg person?" Terrie asked.

"He's the man at church who has had his eye on your sister even before Gerard entered the picture." Betty filled her eldest daughter in.

"Oh, really now?" Terrie raised her thick eyebrows.

"You both need to stop. That man is not interested in me, and I'm certainly not interested in him."

"He is interested in you, but you couldn't see it because you were so in love with Gerard. Back then, you didn't see anything outside of Gerard."

Serena shook her head. "You are too much. I don't think God would have allowed me to marry Gerard only to lead me to Greg."

"Well, Sissy, you do know the story of Jacob and Rachel. That's all I'm saying," Terrie said.

Serena rolled her eyes at her sister. "You both are too much. I can't even believe I'm related to y'all. Mom, are you sure I wasn't adopted?"

They all laughed, and the laughter was cleansing after all the tears.

* * *

Serena felt the ten-day missions trip to Cameroon brought her closer to God, and she received so much pleasure in helping others, but her time out of the country left her with little energy. She had been in bed, sleeping off and on for several days since her return. Still tired, she debated whether she would go to church or rest.

"Serena." Serena sat up in bed and looked around.

"What the—?"

"Serena."

She was sure she had heard her name clearly the second time. She gathered the Louisville Slugger she kept on the side of her bed and went about her loft making sure no one was inside. She double checked all of her locks before returning to her bedroom. She sat on the side of her bed. A shiver spread through her body, and it scared her. It was the same feeling she had experienced a few weeks earlier when she was having brunch with her mother and sister.

"Oh yes, I'm going to church. I've got to rebuke whatever spirit I've brought back from Africa. Satan, I rebuke you in the name of Jesus," she shouted.

At church, Serena found her usual seat with her family. After praise and worship, the pastor walked to the stage. He revved the crowd, and everyone began praising God.

When things quieted, the pastor began his sermon. "Today, we're going to talk about this thing called love. Now everyone who claims to love, really have love. I don't think you hear me now."

"Oh, it is a blessing to give and receive love. True love between a man and woman is sanctified, holy matrimonial love. I didn't make that up. It's right there in your bible. God made Eve for Adam so he would not be alone. Then there's Abram and Sarai. Sarai was barren. She couldn't have children, but she loved Abram so much that she made a child with their servant. Now that may not have been the right way to go about it, but she loved him so much, she gave him the one thing he longed for.

We could talk about Jacob and Rachel and even Ruth and Boaz. Now, I'm preaching to the grown folks today." The pastor shouted, "Love! Will make you do some strange thangs." For forty-five minutes, he continued on with his sermon. Somehow, Serena felt the message was meant for her. She didn't get that feeling too often, but today, while the pastor was preaching, she got that mysterious shiver once again.

"Hello, ladies," Greg Pierce greeted them. Betty and Terrie smiled at each other and left Serena standing there with a man that might as well had been a stranger.

"Hi, Greg. Can I help you with something?" Serena asked politely, checking him out on the sly. She felt guilty for looking at another man in a sinful way and bit the inside of her cheek. Why hadn't she noticed him before? She knew why or maybe she had and didn't want to admit it. Greg was six-feet tall, skin as dark as ebony and had the nerve to have gray eyes. A whiff of his cologne tickled her nose, and she breathed it in. He smelled so good. What was that scent? She tried to put her finger on it while watching his mouth continue to move.

"Issey Miyake," she finally said.

"Excuse me?" Greg asked.

"Oh, I'm sorry," Serena clutched her chest. A moment of awkward silence passed between them, and Serena couldn't remember a more embarrassing time.

Greg cleared his throat. "I was wondering if I could take you out to dinner this weekend?"

"Oh, I'm flattered, but I'm not available this weekend. Sorry."

Greg chuckled. His dimples sent Serena right back into la-la land. "Okay. What about next weekend?"

She shook her head. "Umm, busy then too."

"My, you're one busy lady. Well, how about you check your schedule and give me a call or a text when you have a weekend available." He handed her a business card and turned to walk away. He spun back around. "And yes, it is Issey Miyake," he said, flashing a million-dollar smile.

Serena stood there silently praying. She had no intention of breaking her wedding vows to the man she loved. She went in search of her mother and sister and found them in the church lobby.

"So what day are you going on a date?" Her mother asked.

"Never," Serena said.

"Now I know that boy asked you out. We could tell just by watching."

"Well, he did ask me to dinner, but I told him no."

Terrie looked at her sister. "I hate to bring up Jacob and Rachel again. They did get together, but by the time they did, they were old as dirt. Bloop! I'm going to leave that right there. Meet you two at Baby Does."

Sunday after Sunday, Serena encountered Greg at church. He was persistent, and each Sunday he asked Serena out on a date. After repeatedly rejecting Greg, she surprised everyone—including herself—when she accepted his dinner invitation. She wouldn't have called it a date. She only agreed because he looked like a pathetic little puppy—a begging puppy. And, she thought if she accepted the invitation, it would go wrong and he'd never ask her again.

"And what kind of food does the lady like?" He asked her.

"I'm open," she told him.

"Very well." They finalized dinner plans including the location and time Greg would pick her up at her brother Corey's home. There was no way she would allow him to pick her up at her loft. Besides, she knew if anything went down, Corey would handle it.

"I shall see you Friday at five-thirty. Do you like dancing?"

"No, I have no rhythm."

"Oh, I doubt that," he turned to walk away, but something stopped him.

"And one more thing." He was so close she could smell the cinnamon Altoid on his breath. He leaned into her ear. "God told me that you're going to be my wife." With that, he walked away.

"I'm sorry to inform you, but God did not give me the same revelation," she shouted to his back. But he was gone and did not hear her outburst.

Friday evening, Serena dressed and drove to her brother's home. Greg arrived at five-twenty-five.

"He's prompt," Corey said. "That's important."

Greg rang the doorbell, and Corey opened it. Greg seemed a little confused and thrown off.

"Um, I'm here to pick up...Serena. Maybe I have the wrong address."

"You're at the right place. I'm her brother, Corey. Come on in. Serena will be right down."

After a bit of small talk, Serena appeared, and Greg stood. "You look beautiful," he said.

"Thank you."

"Are you all set?"

"Ready when you are," Serena answered.

They arrived at the Oceanaire Seafood Room, and Serena was impressed. But she got that chilled sensation again. Gerard had brought her here. She loved the food and so had he.

Once they were seated, Greg ordered a bottle of Riesling and started the night off with shrimp and grits. They made small talk, and Serena was able to find out Greg was a retired military vet turned author.

"Why haven't I seen any of your books? I'm an avid reader."

"Perhaps you have. Have you read *Chaos in Baltimore?*"

"Yes, I've read it. It's sitting on my bookshelf."

"That's mine," Greg beamed in pride.

"I thought you were serious," Serena chided. "Ben Abbot wrote that book."

"Tada!" Greg said.

Serena looked confused.

"I write under a pseudonym," he explained.

"Are you serious? Ben—I mean you've written at least two dozen books, and I think I've read all but two."

"Oh, so you're a fan of mine, are you?" He gave her a wicked smile.

"Serena."

"Serena."

Someone was whispering her name. The voice sounded familiar, but she couldn't make it out.

"Serena."

The chill she felt ran rampant through her body.

"Are you okay? You look a little cold. Here, have my jacket." Greg put his suit coat around Serena's shoulders. "All better?"

"Yes. Thank you."

Serena looked around, but no one in the restaurant looked familiar. She didn't want to ask Greg if he had heard her name being called. He would surely think her crazy. Their waiter returned and Greg placed their order, sesame seared wild Hawaiian ahi tuna for Serena and for himself, surf and turf.

They enjoyed their food, and to Serena's surprise, she caught herself enjoying Greg's company. *Nothing serious. Just dinner and conversation between two adults, nothing more.* The conversation flowed, and Serena enjoyed getting to know Greg. She was surprised by all the things she learned about him.

"Let love find you. Give love, receive love."

"What did you say?" Serena asked Greg.

"I didn't say anything, but I am having a wonderful evening."

Serena looked baffled. "Are you sure, because I thought I heard you say something."

"I'm certain," Greg assured her.

"Let love find you. Give love, receive love," the voice said again. Her body began to shiver. The voice that had been calling her was Gerard. "Let love find you. Give love, receive love," were the last words Gerard had said to her.

"Would you like to go dancing? I do a mean salsa."

Serena stood, frozen.

"Or I can take you home. You look like you don't feel well. Should I be concerned or are you not enjoying our date?"

"Let love find you. Give love, receive love."

Serena closed her eyes. People always looked for signs and confirmation and got upset when they missed them, thinking God had not heard them.

She took a deep breath. "Yes. Yes, I'd love to go salsa dancing with you."

Greg closed the passenger door, and Serena looked towards the restaurant and smiled. She tucked the locket Gerard had given her—the one she never took off—inside her dress.

"Let love find you. Give love, receive love," she said with a smile. "I receive that."

About the Author

Her handle is "That Literary Lady," and Yolanda M. Johnson-Bryant wears many hats. She is an author of women's fiction and women's non-fiction, freelance writer, columnist, editor and ghostwriter. In addition, she is a literary, social media, marketing and branding consultant. Yolanda is a literacy and community advocate, as well as a volunteer, Toastmaster and overall geek. In addition to her community volunteer work, Mrs. Johnson-Bryant conducts classes and workshops on literacy, self-publishing, writing, social media, marketing and entrepreneurship.

A Coffee Shop Connection
T. A. Beasley

"Hey, Renee. Wait for me!"

Smiling, Renee stopped and turned.

Karen, her co-worker, offered her a good morning hug. "Girl, I figured I could catch you at Rose's and didn't want to miss you."

"You're just in time." Renee opened the door to Rose's Coffee Café. "You already know I have to have my macchiato before work."

"I know." Karen chuckled. "In five years, your routine has not changed since the first day I met you at our new hire orientation."

After placing their orders, the ladies headed to work at Petra's Wellness Salon and Spa with coffee drinks in hand. At the corner of 86th and Westfield Blvd, Renee nudged Karen to get her attention. "Girl, look at that handsome man helping the elderly lady with her cart across the street. Now that's a quality I want in a man."

"Who are you talking about?" Karen looked around, trying to trace Renee's gaze.

"See the guy helping the little old lady across the street?" Renee pointed in the man's direction.

"Aww, that is sweet, and he is cute. Wow!"

Renee giggled. "I know, right? We better go before we're late."

* * *

Davis Brock made a point to walk down College Street to work. He had a feeling Mrs. Brooks would try to cross the street to go to the store. It worried him that she tried to push her shopping cart to the store alone – despite his warnings. He glanced at his watch, checking to see how late he would be. Brandy, his office manager, would have to open the coffee shop and handle things for him. He pulled out his cellphone to give her a heads up just as Mrs. Brooks stopped near the corner by the Steak-N-Shake.

"Good morning, Mrs. Brooks. Let me help you across," he offered, slightly breathless from dashing to catch her. Davis was afraid she might injure herself. He took hold of her cart and placed her hand in the crook of his arm. Mrs. Brooks and her husband used to come into his coffee shop to read newspapers. Davis has enjoyed their company, as did everyone else who stopped by the shop, but Mrs. Brooks stopped coming after her husband passed.

"Thank you for your help, Davis."

"You're welcome, Mrs. Brooks. Can you make it? Or would you like me to go with you?"

Mrs. Brooks placed her hand on her hip and gave him a hard look. "Son, I've been going to this drugstore since before you were born. Now, get to work!" She swatted him on the bottom.

Davis laughed and kissed her cheek. "I'm going, I'm going, but please be careful." He watched her a little longer then turned in the direction of his coffee shop.

He opened the door and Brandy was running things like a pro. "Thanks." He squeezed her shoulders. "I don't know what I'd do without you."

"You got delayed by Mrs. Brooks, didn't you?" She asked.

"You know I don't like her trying to walk to the store by herself."

Brandy smiled before turning to stock the cabinets. "She's stubborn and just because you live in the same area doesn't mean you're responsible for her."

"Well, she made that very clear this morning. Even gave me a swat on the behind," Davis laughed. He walked into his office and grabbed an apron. The next busy wave of customers was upon them.

* * *

The next day, Renee rushed out her door running a little late. She stopped at Rose's for coffee, but the line was out the door. A glance at her watch told her she didn't have time to wait. *I'll just have to drink that nasty coffee at the salon.* She started in the direction of the spa, but a sign for Brock's Coffee Shop caught her attention.

"I bet they have a macchiato." She looked at her watch again. "You know what, I should have enough time." Renee ran across the street and entered the shop. She'd never been in this coffee shop before. She glanced around, taking in the atmosphere. The shop was tastefully decorated with soothing colors and pops of art on the wall. There was a cozy sitting area for conversation and a counter height bar for internet use. Renee made her way to the ordering counter.

"Welcome to Brock's Coffee Shop. What can I get for you today?"

Renee perused the menu. "I'd like a large salted caramel macchiato."

"Your name for the order."

Renee told the cashier her name and paid for her coffee. With a smile, the cashier told her where to pick up her coffee. Renee loved the customer service. She thanked the cashier and stepped to the side to wait for her order. She looked at her phone to see how much time she had.

"I have a salted caramel macchiato for...Renee?"

Renee looked for the deep, sexy voice calling her name. She approached the counter to pick up her coffee and came face to face with the gentleman she had seen helping the elderly lady cross the street. She couldn't stop staring at him.

"Renee? Your drink." He waved the cup back and forth in front of her, drawing her from her trance.

"Thanks," she said, reaching for the cup. "Wait, how did you know my name?"

"It's on your name tag," he smiled at her. "Plus, the cashier always writes each customer's first name on their cup. We take pride in not getting our customers' drinks mixed up."

Renee looked at her name tag. "Hmm. Well, thanks for my coffee. You're a lifesaver."

"You're welcome, and Renee?"

She turned around. "Yes?"

"If I were you, I wouldn't throw that cup away." He winked then looked down at the next cup. He called the next customer, and Renee turned to make her way out the door. With only five minutes to spare, she power walked the last two blocks to work thinking about what the handsome man had said about the cup. She sat the cup down on her desk and turned it around. *Davis Brock, 317-868-1652, Call me sometime* was written on the side of the cup. Renee couldn't help but chuckle. She wondered if he did that to all the females who came into his coffee shop. It was apparent he was the owner. His picture, name, and a brief history of the shop were printed on the back of the cup.

Of all the days for Karen to be off, it happened to be the one day Renee met her dream guy. She couldn't wait for their lunch break tomorrow. This would be a great conversation piece.

Over the next couple of weeks, Davis and Renee talked on the phone every evening. She learned about his break up and how he came to own the coffee shop. She was intrigued that he had overcome depression to run a successful business. Davis told her it had been a year since he'd dated anyone and assured her he didn't make it a habit of putting his name and number on the side of coffee cups. She shared about her love of coffee, reading, exploring, her obsession with organizing, and her fears about falling in love and being hurt.

"I feel like I've known you forever," he told her one evening on a late-night call.

"I feel the same way, Davis."

He cleared his throat. "I'd like to cook dinner for you and maybe we can watch a movie together."

"Are you suggesting a date?"

"I guess I am. Would you be open to dinner and a movie with me?"

She blushed, glad he couldn't see her. "Davis, I thought you'd never ask. I would love to have dinner and a movie with you."

"You've made my night, Renee. Until tomorrow at seven p.m., pretty lady, I bid you good night."

"Goodnight, Davis." Renee ended the call with a big cheesy grin. Thankful, yet again that he could not see her, she sighed and fell back on her bed. The sound of his voice and the way he said her name made her want to spend a lifetime with him. She felt safe with Davis and appreciated that he wasn't rushing her into anything. *Davis Brock is a keeper.*

* * *

Renee sat beside Karen at lunch. "You could have waited for me," she teased Karen.

"Girl, you were taking too long," Karen bit into her sandwich. "I was starving. Besides, those invoices will be there when we get back."

"You're right, but I need to leave work on time today." Renee sipped from her drink then unwrapped her sandwich.

"You're the only person I know who has a process for eating her food." Karen picked up her fruit cup.

"Excuse me for making sure I digest my food, Miss Gobble-My-Food-Down-in-Five-Seconds." Renee ate a spoonful of her soup, then bit into the corner of her sandwich.

"You're also the only person I know who cuts off the edges of the bread on her sandwich." Karen laughed. "Who does that?"

"I can't help it. I'm scared they will choke me."

"Girl, that's nonsense." Karen shook her head. "Tell me about your lover, Davis. How is it going with you two?"

"First of all, he is not my lover. We are getting to know each other before taking the next step."

"How long does getting to know take? You two have been talking for months. You've had several dates. How much more time do you need?"

"We aren't rushing anything. Besides, it's better to wait and let the anticipation build."

"You're full of it, Renee. How long has it been since you had a strong man like Davis wrap his arms around you and make you feel like a woman again?"

Renee pinched her friend. "Girl, get your mind out of the gutter and let's get back to work."

Later at her home, Renee thought about her conversation with Karen while preparing dinner for Davis. She felt comfortable with Davis, and she loved the way he made her laugh. But she wanted to wait until marriage for intimacy, and Davis didn't seem to have a problem with that. He encouraged her to be her true self with him - whether goofy or serious. She placed the last dish on the dining room table just as the doorbell rang. She looked at herself in the hallway mirror, smoothing down her maxi skirt and adjusting her blouse. She flipped her long black hair over her shoulder and went to the door.

"Davis, I hope you're hungry." She teased with a beaming smile. But it wasn't Davis. Renee's smile vanished as she stared at the police officer.

"Hello, ma'am. I'm Officer Ellis with the Indianapolis Police Department." He extended his hand toward her as if offering a handshake.

Renee frowned and clasped her hands protectively in front of her, leaving the officer's pre-offered hand hanging in the air. "Hello, what can I do for you?"

The officer stepped sideways. The aroma of food wafted through the open door. "Did I catch you at a bad time?"

"No. What can I do for you, Officer?" Renee asked again, uncrossing and crossing her arms, unsure of where to put them.

"Are you related to a Davis Brock?"

Renee's heart sunk. "Yes and no. I mean, we're dating." She teetered, feeling lightheaded. "What is going on?"

The officer gently grabbed her arm. "Whoa. Steady there. How about you sit down, and then I'll explain? Mr. Brock listed you as his next of kin."

"He did? Wait, what happened to Davis?" Renee felt anxious. She clutched her stomach.

"He's been in an accident, and we'd like you to accompany us to the hospital."

She stood, grabbed her purse, and allowed the officer to lead her out of the house. Within fifteen minutes, Renee walked through the emergency room doors at Saint Vincent hospital. Her hands trembled with fear. She had no idea what she was walking into or what had happened to Davis, but she was trying to keep it together.

The officer led her to the counter. "Hello, Miss. I'm Officer Ellis. I have Renee Spencer here with me. Mr. Brock has been asking for her." The lady nodded and picked up the phone.

A nurse appeared. "Right this way, mam."

Renee turned to the detective and thanked him for his help then followed the nurse through the double doors and down a hallway to a room with curtains drawn.

"Mr. Brock, you have a visitor," the nurse announced, pulling the curtain back enough for Renee to slip through.

Renee rushed toward the hospital bed. "Davis, oh my God! What happened to you?" Tears welled in her eyes, and Davis reached up to wipe them away.

Before he could say anything, the nurse said, "Your name was the first one he called when he woke up. I'll leave you two to visit."

"Renee, I'm sorry I worried you," Davis said.

"That you did." She swiped at her face. "Imagine my surprise when a cop showed up at my door instead of you."

He laughed a little. "Please don't make me laugh. It hurts."

Renee placed his hand in hers and raised it to her cheek. "I was terrified. I thought you were gone. I wanted to ask God why he would give you to me and then take you away."

"Well, for one, never question what God is or isn't doing to you or for you. He knows exactly what He is doing."

Renee nodded her head. "I know. I caught myself before it left my lips."

Davis ran his hand down the length of her hair. "I should have thought about it before trying to be a hero."

"A hero? What do you mean?"

"I was walking to your house when I saw Mrs. Brooks trying to cross the street heading toward the library. She was struggling with her bag, so I went to help." He winced and changed positions. "I got her across the street safely, but on my way back, a car didn't stop at the red light. It hit me as it turned the corner, hence the broken leg and arm in a sling."

"Davis, you could have been killed! Don't ever scare me like that again. I was a nervous wreck on the way here." Renee kissed his forehead.

"I'm going to be okay, just banged up a little. If they were going any faster, it probably would have killed me."

"How did the cops know where I lived?"

"I'm an only child. My parents are deceased. I have no one else who would be worried about me, except maybe Brandy when I didn't show to open the store in the morning. I didn't want you waiting on me for dinner, so I told them where to find you." He looked away for a moment before returning his attention towards her. "Besides, you're the only one I wanted to be here with me."

Renee touched her forehead to his. "There's no place I'd rather be, Davis. Thank you."

The doctor released Davis after a couple of days of observation, and Renee prepared lunch for his homecoming since they never got to have dinner. She made sure his leg and arm were comfortable then helped him with his food.

"I'm so glad you walked into my coffee shop."

"I'm glad I did too." She kissed him on the cheek. "And I'm especially glad I didn't throw away that cup."

They both laughed.

* * *

Two Years Later

Davis called Karen. "Is she with you?"

"Yes, *Mom*. I know what I'm doing." Karen teased him.

"Everything is in place. Be here in ten minutes."

"Got it. I'll be sure to stop by."

"Take your places, everyone." Davis clapped his hands together. Friends and family hid behind the couch, the curtains in the living room and some hid in the hallway closet.

Flowers in hand, he positioned himself on the stairs where Renee would see him when Karen brought her through the door. Beads of perspiration slid down his forehead, but he resisted the urge to fidget. He nestled the flowers in the crook of his arm and patted his pocket. The precious item was still there. He wanted this moment to be perfect. Where was she? He was trying not to let his nerves get to him. "Dang, ten minutes is taking forever!"

Brandy, his trusted employee, peeked out from behind the curtain. "Would you please be still? You're making the rest of us nervous." The ripple of laughter quieted as keys turned in the lock.

Davis wiped the sweat from his brow and looked toward the door. Brandy repositioned the curtain to hide her silhouette and Davis froze at attention like a soldier keeping watch. Karen and Renee entered the house, laughing. Everyone jumped out from their hiding places. "Surprise!" They all yelled in unison.

Renee placed a hand to her chest and gasped. Eyes wide from the commotion, her vision landed on the staircase. Davis descended the stairs and walked towards her. He placed the flowers in her hands and, without taking his eyes off hers, kneeled on one knee.

Renee took him in, absorbing the moment. Davis was attired in one of her favorite outfits, his gray and teal pinstripe suit with a teal tie and soft gray Stacy Adams. She placed her free hand over her mouth to cover the scream building in her lungs and buried her face in the fragrant flowers to hide the tears forming in the corners of her eyes. This was all so surreal. Now, she understood why Karen was acting so strange.

"Get it done, Davis!" Brandy called out.

Davis wiped his forehead once more and gulped. "Renee, since the first day you walked into my coffee shop, I knew there was something special about you. Over the last two years, you have laughed with me, cried with me, churched with me, listened to me, loved me, and taken care of me as a wife would. I don't want to be on a beach, a plane, or in a house unless you're with me. Renee Elaine Spencer, will you marry me?" Davis took the ring out of his pocket and opened the black box. He held it up to her with a hopeful look, waiting for an answer.

Renee passed the bouquet of flowers to Karen and held out her left hand to accept the ring.

Brandy leaned over to Renee's aunt. "Does this mean she said yes?"

For the first time, Renee looked around the room at their family and friends gathered there. She smiled and looked back at Davis. "Yes! A million times, yes. Yes, I'll marry you, Davis Alexander Brock!"

He slid the ring on her finger then scooped her up in a bear hug and swung her around. "I love you," he told Renee before placing her back on her feet.

"I love you, Davis." She looked up at him. "I'm really glad I came into your coffee shop."

He leaned in to his fiancée. "And, I'm glad you answered when I called your name." Davis sealed the moment with a kiss as family and friends cheered on.

About the Author

T. A. Beasley is an author, blogger and book reviewer, who loves all things literary. Her love for books prompted her to start *Authors & Readers Book Corner*, a blog that supports authors by sharing their books with readers. She is the author of *It Happened To Me* and founder of LaBrice Books. Beasley resides in Indianapolis, Indiana, with her husband.

A Timeless Love
Naa Harper

1998

"Ha, ha, ha!" Bursts of laughter erupted from across the street. My best friend, Valerie Duncan and her little brother Ricky teased me mercilessly, yelling out the kissing song.

Candace and Michael sitting in the tree
K-i-s-s-i-n-g
First comes love.
Then comes marriage.
Then comes baby in the baby carriage,
Sucking his thumb,
Wetting his pants,
Doing the hula, hula dance

"Stop it," I yelled, visibly shaken by their silly taunts. I hoped nobody noticed how my knees shook uncontrollably, I was already embarrassed.

How could Valerie do this to me? She of all people knew how I felt about being teased in front of people.

We ran as fast as we could across the busy street towards Commerce Road and Zion Hill. A blue beat up Chevrolet sedan with a cracked windshield and one working headlight missed hitting us by a few inches. Our feet abruptly hit the cracked sidewalk.

Michael and I made a mad dash to Sam's Corner Market, a safe place for us to catch our breath. Only a half a block away from school, most of the kids from Olive High showed little remorse about stealing candy bars, potato chips, and sodas from the little corner store.

Michael and I made our way into the back of Mr. Sam's store where no one could see us. It was not the most romantic place to hide, but for the moment, I was far removed from my friend's merciless teasing. And, being with Michael was really all that mattered.

At six foot one inches, he was dark like a piece of To'ak chocolate with curly brown hair. The smell of his cologne took my breath away. He also happened to be the most handsome guy at Olive High and the star quarterback of the football team. At seventeen, all ninety-five pounds of my five-foot three-inch frame adored Michael Taylor. He was not only handsome and athletic, he was smart and had a kind soul.

As we lingered in the back of Sam's Corner Market, Michael and I gasped for air trying to catch our breath.

"Whew! I'm tired," I huffed.

Michael gently wrapped his arms around my body.

"Michael? What are you—"

Before I could finish, he landed a big wet kiss on my lips. "Candace, I love you."

The sound of his words was music to my ears. "I love you too."

I knew love was a strong and complicated word, but it summed up how I felt about Michael. Granted, I was seventeen and an only child. Everything I'd learned about love, I saw on television or read in romance novels. My parents rarely showed any affection towards one another. They argued more than they kissed and, for most of my childhood, slept in separate beds, so a girl learned where she could.

"Excuse me." I pulled myself from Michael's grip, catching a glimpse of my watch. "I need to get home, Michael. It's almost four o'clock. Mu mom will have my head if I don't get my homework and chores done."

He raised his hands in mock surrender. "Hey, I get it. It's our senior year of high school. I'm not gonna argue with Mom; everything matters."

I grimaced, but inside I was smiling. *He always gets me. This is why I'm in love.*

"How's the calculus going? Wanna talk tonight and go over the answers to our homework over the phone?"

I shook my head. "Can't, I told Valerie I would call her later tonight, and you know Mom only allows one phone call on a school night. I just hope and pray Mr. Sturbaum will show some amount pity on me when he grades my final math exam. Calculus is just not my cup of tea."

Michael wrapped his arm around my shoulder. "Ah, don't be so hard on yourself. I'm sure you did fine. We're gonna go to Broward and be superstars, you watch."

I smiled. Going to college at Broward University had been my dream ever since I was a little girl. No one in my family, on either side, had gone to college. I would be a first generation college student. I often visualized myself walking across the stage at my college commencement to waves of loud applause as my name, "Candace Taylor," was announced to everyone in attendance. What a wonderful day it would be and one I thought about every day.

"Earth to Candace. Where'd you go?" Michael waved his hand in front of my face as if he were waking me from some sort of trance.

I blinked. "Daydreaming about calculus and college, I guess. Who knows? I should head home, so I can do my homework and help Momma with dinner."

Michael reached for my hand. "Okay, well let's not keep Momma waiting."

Later that evening, while finishing my chores, I thought about our kiss and the college plans I had made with my high school sweetheart. We both lived in Oak Forest, a racially mixed neighborhood in small town Farmville, but relocating to Washington D.C., living in a big city, attending Broward University, a historically Black university, would be new and different. It's what we both wanted, and we were excited. Perhaps it was the freedom we would have to be together and do whatever we wanted. The possibilities were endless.

I completed my homework, and called Valerie. Prom was two weeks away, and we were scheming. We giggled endlessly thinking of ways we could get our dates at the same table for the evening.

"What are you most excited about?" Valerie asked.

"Everything," I said. "Prom is going to be a night to remember."

Little did I know how true those words would be.

Olive High Prom Night

I couldn't believe this was my last high school prom, and I was going with the handsome, intelligent, athletic, Michael Taylor. *Eat your heart out, America. I've caught the prize.* I looked in the mirror and grinned the silliest grin. My strapless fuchsia sweetheart dress gracefully covered my petite frame.

"Come, Candace. Let's get your hair and makeup done." I heard Momma yell.

"Yes, mam," I yelled back. I gave the bathroom mirror one last silly grin and walked into my bedroom.

Momma sat the hairbrush she was holding on the bed when I came in the room. She embraced me, then stood back with her hands on my shoulders. "Oh, Candace. You're beautiful! Your father and I are so proud of you. I know tonight is going to be amazing."

"Thank you, Momma." My palms were sweaty and my stomach was somewhat empty from not eating all day. I had worried that if I ate too much, my dress would not fit. I wanted tonight to be perfect.

"I can't believe you're about to graduate high school and go off to college." Momma picked up the hairbrush and styled my hair in a perfect bun.

I looked at myself in the mirror, seeing so much of her in me. The resemblance was scary.

"Here, let's put some blush on your cheekbones." I could feel Momma's love for me as she applied my makeup. "Okay," she smiled, "stand back and let me get a good look at you."

I stepped back and posed, then twirled around. We both laughed at my antics.

"Should we go down and take a few pictures while you for Michael? It's six o'clock. He should be arriving shortly." Momma said.

I went downstairs, thinking about how handsome Michael would look in his white tuxedo. He'd chosen a fuchsia cummerbund to match my dress. I was so anxious waiting for Michael to arrive that droplets of perspiration formed under my armpits.

Noise pierced the waiting. The shrill sound of sirens could be heard in the distance. The disturbing noise sounded like it was about two blocks away. I looked out the window. "Momma, do you hear that?"

She came into the living room. "Yes, it sounds like an ambulance. Here, come sit with me on the sofa."

I couldn't explain the dis-ease. I had no idea going to the prom could make me feel so anxious. I leaned back against the sofa and closed my eyes, envisioning Michael and I dancing the night away.

When six turned into seven o'clock, I was praying my makeup would hold up along with my feet, which were already starting to hurt. I had promised Valerie that Michael and I would meet her in the hotel lobby at seven thirty. Michael was never late, but I didn't want to assume the worst. Maybe he just needed a few extra minutes to get ready, I knew he liked to look nice.

Fifteen more minutes went by and I began to worry. Would we have time to take some pictures together before we left? Had he stood me up?

I walked back to the living room window. "Momma, did the phone ring?"

"No, baby, the phone hasn't rang."

I wasn't sure what to do. The prom had officially started.

At eight o'clock, tired of waiting and wondering, I called Michael's house. But there was no answer. I called Valerie to see if I could catch a ride with her, but her mother said she had already left. Tears filled my eyes as

I quietly went into my room and sat on the edge of my bed.

"Candace? Candace, where are you?" Momma called.

"Upstairs," I yelled. "In my bedroom."

"Are you alright?" Momma asked.

"Momma, It's after eight. Michael didn't show. Should I get out of my dress? Should I call his house to see where he is?"

Momma squeezed my hand. "I think that would be a good idea."

I dialed Michael's house with Momma sitting close by.

"Hello, Mrs. Taylor?"

"No, this is not Mrs. Taylor." The voice on the other end said. "This is Thelma, the housekeeper. How can I help you?"

"Umm, Ms. Thelma. This is Candace, Michael's girlfriend. He was supposed to pick me up for prom at seven, but he hasn't arrived yet."

Silence filled the line. I looked at Momma with tears in my eyes. "Hello?"

My mom grabbed the phone. "Hi, this is Evelyn, Candace's mom. We're concerned about Michael. Is everything okay?"

I watched Momma's hand fly to her mouth. "Oh, dear God," she said. "I'm... We're... Thank you for letting us know."

Momma hung up the phone and turned towards me, her mouth pinched in pain. "Honey, I am so sorry. It seems... It seems Michael was on his way to pick you up and had a head-on collision with a drunk driver. Candace, he was killed on impact."

I flew into Momma's arms, screaming at the top of my lungs. "Nooooo! Oh my God! Oh my God! Nooooo! Please, God. Noooooo!"

Everything after that moment is hazy. Somehow I managed to live with a heavy heart from that proclamation to the following week when I attended Michael's funeral. I emotionally faded in and out of the funeral service. I remember the words *Always loved... never forgotten... forever missed...* were engraved on his tombstone and on my heart.

After Michael's death, I fell into a deep depression, unable to sleep, barely able to eat. I lost fifteen pounds. It took months for me to realize he was never coming back. I was devastated, and at seventeen, this unexpected loss caused me to never want to fall in love again. *The loss was too much.*

They say love only comes once in a lifetime. Right?

The emotional pain I suffered from Michael's death was, at times, more than I could handle. Even though I was grieving, I still needed to consider my future. How would I make it? How was I supposed to live without Michael? What would I do now? What was my next step? College had been the next step for both Michael and I for as long as I could remember.

Despite the devasting loss that I would not wish on my worst enemy, I managed to graduate from Olive High and received a full scholarship to Broward University. By the end of the summer, Momma and I drove to Washington D.C. She and Daddy had separated the day of Michael's funeral, adding more pain to my life.

I attended Broward University for four years and graduated at the top of my class with a degree in

Business Administration. Going to college, in spite of my grief, was one of the best decisions I ever made.

2018
New Friendships

After graduating from Broward University's business school, I landed a director position with a nonprofit organization helping single mothers improve their economic and academic skills through entrepreneur programs and GED classes. It was a dream position for me because my momma never made it past the tenth grade. She wasn't dumb or incapable of completing her studies. In fact, my momma was an amazing woman, but unfavorable family circumstances had caused her to become a high school dropout. With this position, I was helping women like my momma.

Living in Washington D.C., was a blessing. At thirty-six, I felt like my life was finally on track. I owned a home in the Mount Pleasant area of Washington, D.C., not far from the downtown business district. I loved living in Mount Pleasant's eclectic, quiet residential neighborhood with easy access to transit. I could easily travel to work, the farmers market and Heller's Bakery for some of the best cupcakes and baked goods in town. All of these positive attributes kept me from running back home to Farmville and old memories.

I was by no means desperate for a man, but no matter what I tried, be it speed dating or online dating, things never seemed to work out. I had reached a very pivotal point in my career and even though all of my hard work had afforded me opportunities and experiences I would never want to trade, there was still something missing. I wanted companionship. I wanted to have intelligent conversations and someone of the opposite sex to laugh at my jokes. But at my age, the dating scene was not so good.

It was hard enough hearing Momma ask, "When are you going to get married?" The pressure was too much. I still believed what God had for me was for me. Despite Momma's inquiring mind about my relationship status, I knew she was proud of all I had accomplished. Being the director of a major nonprofit had been a blessing and a lot of hard work. Late hours and sometimes working from home on the weekends paid off. Plus, my work allowed me to travel and help Momma who was now retired.

Momma wasn't the only one concerned about me dating, so was Anita, my neighbor and friend. And I was trying to keep a straight face as I listened to her extol the merits of the the old school way of dating.

"I'm just saying, Candace, with all of these fake personalities on social media these days, face to face is the way to meet your guy." Anita had stopped by to invite me over to dinner but never missed an opportunity to encourage me to get in the game.

"Anita, I hear you. I do. And for the most part, I agreed with you. But in this day and age, folks are just more about themselves and what they can get. Sometimes it's hard to see the light at the end of the tunnel."

"Girl, what's with this pity party? You can't give up. There are gentlemen who are still gentlemen. You're on vacation for the next two weeks. What are you planning to do?"

I shook my head. If it was one thing I could say about Anita, she was persistent...and a little bossy. "I'm going to unwind and have some fun, and not be stressed out about trying to meet a man. Besides, Momma, my friend Valerie and her nine-year-old son, Gafton are coming to spend some time with me."

I had this big ole house, three bedroom, two and a half baths. It was a great tax write off but pretty lonely with no one to help me fill the space.

"Well, I'm sure you're looking forward to their company. Bring them with you to dinner. I love feeding people."

"That's kind of you, Anita. I know they would love to meet you." I turned towards my door. "I should go. I'm exhausted. The last day at work before vacation is always long and tedious for me."

"Oh, girl. I didn't mean to be inconsiderate. I completely understand work taking a toll. Let me let you—"

Before Anita could finish, my cell phone rang.

She gestured for me to take the call and waved good-bye.

I mouthed good-bye to my neighbor while answering the phone and unlocking the door to my home. "Hey, Val. What's up?"

"Hey, girl. We should be there around nine in the morning."

"Okay, I'll see you all in the morning. Be safe on the road." I dragged myself into the house. All I wanted to do was take a hot shower and go to bed.

Heart racing, I jumped out of bed and threw on an old pair of shorts and my favorite Broward t-shirt. It was 8:30 A.M. and my family would be knocking on my front door at any minute.

I looked at the clothes and shoes strewn around my bedroom. Thankfully, it was the only room in the house that was a mess. The other bedrooms and bathrooms were intact. Living the single life had some advantages.

The sound of a car pulling into the driveway told me they were here. Adrenaline ran through my body.

"Candace!" Valerie yelled as she slammed the car door.

I nearly tripped over my own two feet running down the porch steps. "Hey, everybody!" I yelled, throwing my arms around Valerie. It had been too long since we'd seen one another.

"Mmmph! What am I chopped liver?" asked Momma.

I laughed. She could be so extra at times. "I'm sorry, Momma. I didn't mean to ignore you."

"I know, baby. I was just messing with you." Momma pulled me into a hug.

Gafton sat in the backseat entranced by his iPad.

"Gafton, aren't you going to get out of the car and give your god mommy a hug?"

Gafton exited the vehicle with a sigh and went back to looking at his iPad.

"Here, let me help y'all with your luggage. How was the drive?"

"We made good time," Valerie said.

"Sure, did," my momma added. "Thankfully, we didn't have too much traffic. So, what you got cooked up for us to get into while we're here?"

"Well, speaking of cooking. My friend, Anita invited us to her place for dinner."

Valerie, Gafton, Momma and I joined Anita and a few others for dinner. We were enjoying a game of bingo when the doorbell rang.

"I'll get it." Anita jumped up to answer the door.

"Hey, Walter! Glad you could make it." I heard her call out. I turned my attention back to the bingo game until Anita returned to the living room with an intelligent looking man in glasses. He had such a serious look on his face, I wondered what he did for a living.

"Hey everyone, meet Walter, my little brother." Anita said to all of us.

"Hello, everyone, nice to meet you all." Walter said.

After a chorus of hellos, Anita encouraged Walter to join the crowd. "I'm going to bring the food out while you all finish your game," she said before slipping back into the kitchen.

Walter looked around for a place to sit.

"Please, sit here." I offered.

"Oh, thanks... I'm sorry what was your name?" Walter smiled.

The look on Valerie's face made me want to laugh. She looked real pleased to see Anita's brother sitting next to me. I winked at Valerie, and then smiled at Walter. "Yes. I'm Candace."

"Candace, what a beautiful name." He said.

"Thank you." I replied.

Valerie won bingo for the fifth time, and Momma said she was tired of losing so she went to the kitchen to offer Anita some assistance.

"Wash your hands, everyone," Anita yelled from the kitchen. "Time to eat."

When Anita, spoke everyone listened.

"Before we eat, let's have a moment of prayer," Anita didn't wait for our assent. "Father, we thank you for this evening and the food we are about to eat. Thank you for our friends who have come from Virginia and for Walter. Amen."

Everyone said, "Amen."

We ate baked chicken, a fresh Caesar salad, fried fish, macaroni and cheese and red velvet cupcakes until our hearts and bellies were content. The rest of the evening was spent talking about politics, weather and other random things until it was time to leave.

Walter hugged his sister and took out his keys. "Dinner was fantastic, Sis."

"Thanks, Walter. I'm glad you enjoyed it." Anita said.

"Thanks for having us over," I said.

Walter took my hand and kissed it. "Goodnight, Candace," he said. "It was lovely to meet you."

Flustered, I said, "It was a pleasure meeting you as well, Walter."

I'd met a gentleman face to face. And while I didn't think he was trying to be anything but a gentleman, the stars in the D.C. sky were beautiful. On a night like this, anything was possible.

I laid in bed thinking about Walter and how much we had in common. During dinner, he mentioned he was president of a kids club. I found it interesting that we both were in the same field of helping people. I wondered if he was in a relationship.

Before I could turn off the lamp, my phone rang. *Who in the world was calling me this late at night?* I reached for the phone. "Hello."

"Hello. Candace?"

I did not recognize the voice on the other end. "Who is this?"

"It's me, Walter."

I swallowed hard to move the lump in my throat. Could this really be happening? "Umm. Hi, Walter."

"I hope you don't mind me calling this late. Nita gave me your phone number."

"No, I don't mind. But I am a little shocked." I felt like an awkward young girl talking to her crush on the phone for the first time.

"You've been on my mind since I left my sister's house. I'd love to know more about you."

His voice was so calming.

"Would you be interested in talking on the phone with me every once in a while and maybe grabbing a bite to eat sometime?"

"I'd like that, Walter."

He sighed as if he'd been holding his breath. "Great! Well, why don't you check your schedule for this Friday night? Maybe we can grab a bite to eat around seven."

I agreed to meet Walter on Friday and called Anita.

She answered on the first ring. "Please tell me you aren't mad that I gave my brother your phone number without permission."

"I'm not mad, but Anita, you totally set me up!"

She chuckled. "I didn't do anything except invite two single people to my home for dinner and let a gentleman be a gentleman."

"Okay, you got me," I laughed. "Have a good night, neighbor. I'm going to bed."

How could I be upset with her? I was more thankful than anything, and not because a man was interested in me. I was thankful God had given me another chance to have a new relationship. Michael had been gone for a long time and my heart was finally in a place where it was healed.

Walter picked me up on Friday, looking handsome in a black polo shirt and skinny jeans. We headed to Jaro's restaurant in Dupont Circle for sushi. The hostess seated us in a cozy booth at the front of the restaurant near the windows. Finally, we were seeing one another up close and personal. Both of us were middle aged with hints of gray scattered throughout the natural color of our hair. Our undefined waist lines and love for food were two things Walter and I had in common.

Walter placed his iPhone on the table. "How long have you been coming to this place?"

I took a sip from my glass of water. "About two years."

He nodded. "The same amount of time I've been eating sushi."

I laughed. "I'm a country girl from Virginia in case you didn't know."

"I did not know, but I'm glad you told me," Walter chuckled. "I didn't grow up eating sushi either, to be quite honest. I'm from D.C. My parents split when I was five and my mom moved to Baltimore with my grandparents. She took me with her."

Baltimore was one of my old stomping grounds with Valerie. "So, you know all about Faidley's Seafood and their dynamite crab cakes?"

Walter sat back and smiled. "Look at you knowing something about my hometown. I'm impressed."

Our conversation flowed effortlessly, and I enjoyed looking into his natural green eyes while feasting on a spicy tuna roll. We spent three hours at Jaro's listening to the local jazz group. I enjoyed and silently watched Walter as he ate temaki.

Walter sat back against the booth. "The food is delicious here. I can't believe I'm going to have to take the rest of this temaki home."

Walter helped me with my coat, and I smiled. "I'm glad you enjoyed my spot. I enjoyed being with you."

He returned the smile. "We should plan to do this again, Candace. Soon."

I nodded, feeling my cheeks warm at the thought of spending another evening with him. I prayed for many more lovely evenings.

It had been a long time since a good man like Walter called my name, but it was not too late to for love. After losing Michael and believing for so long that love would never come around again, I was grateful that love called my name.

About the Author

Naa Harper is a Christian speaker, author, and Bible teacher. She's written two books, *After* and *Living Your Dreams: A Woman's Guide to Fulfilling Her Destiny*. Naa is also a wife, and mother, which is one of her first loves. Her other love is sharing messages of hope, faith, and overcoming through the Word of God. She loves to speak about leadership, parenting, teen development, and God being the solution for everything.

One Day I'll Be Gone
Leslie K. Howard

Chapter 1

"She's gone. She's gone. My Jenny is gone," Tom sobbed bitterly on the pastor's shoulder. Tom could hear Pastor Clemons praying, "Jesus, how can I relieve his grief?" Tom had never felt so broken. It was like being a helpless child seeking comfort in his father's strong arms. "I-I r-r-remember the day you married us, Pastor." Tom stuttered hoarsely while looking at the large stain of tears and snot he had left on the man's shirt. "Now, she's gone. My sweet Jenny is gone."

Tom and Jeanette met five years ago, but he remembered it like it was yesterday. Sunday, May 23, 1970, Tom stood at the mirror smiling approvingly at his image. He wore his gray Botany 500 suit with his black wide brimmed hat tilted on right side of his head and thought to himself, "I look good". "Yes," he said aloud while adjusting his black tie to lay in the center of his crisp white shirt. He firmly believed in standing out from the crowd. Most of his friends had dirty jobs like garbage men, grease monkeys or janitors, but Tom was a mail clerk at the Post Office. He had a "good" government job and sometimes liked to dress the part. Someone told him a long time ago that you never get a second chance to make a first impression and today, he intended to live up to that mantra.

"What you all dressed up for man?" Paul, his roommate asked.

"I'm going to church," Tom responded.

"Church?" Paul exclaimed, almost choking on his coffee. "Aren't you afraid of lightning striking you or something?"

"Nah, man," Tom laughed. "Hughes invited me. There's a cookout afterwards. It starts at noon, so I'll get to church around 11:45."

Paul shook his head in disbelief and they both laughed as Tom headed out the door.

* * *

Jeanette was a meek, quiet woman who never raised her voice as long as you didn't cross her too many times. She and her two friends were assigned to serve vegetables at the Christian Missionary Church's annual cookout. The three stood behind a table, Mary at one end serving candied yams, Stacy at the other doling out collard greens while Jeanette, assigned to the summer corn, was stationed in the middle. Jeanette smiled, cheerfully greeting each person as they passed through the serving line. It was then that she first saw him.

After forty-five minutes of manning her station, her feet began to hurt. She craned her neck to see how many were waiting to be served. *One, two... eight, nine ten, eleven... fourteen*, she silently counted. *Great*, she thought to herself while smiling. *Almost finished.* Her eyes trailed back over the line of people and locked with a stranger.

The handsome man gazed at her and smiled, nodding his head in acknowledgement. Jeanette realized she was still smiling and quickly stopped. She felt flush and slightly embarrassed that a stranger caught her looking at him. *Was he watching me all along? What must he think of me? Why do I care what he thinks? He doesn't even know me.*

"Girl, look how much corn you putting on my plate," Mother Jones' rebuke broke Jeanette's reverie. "You know we don't need to be wasting no food around here. We have to be diligent stewards of what the good Lord gives us."

"I'm sorry, Mother." Jeanette said flustered. "I know. I just... I wasn't paying attention to what I was doing."

Mother Jones pursed her lips. "Well, I'll just give this plate to my son so it doesn't go to waste. He'll make my plate. Be more careful next time, you hear?"

Jeanette smiled sheepishly as Mother Jones stormed off.

Before long, the stranger Jeanette had spied from a distance was standing in front of her. She could tell he was checking her out. She touched the cluster of curls dangling from her pinned up hair. His presence made her so nervous that she failed to greet him as she did the others before him.

"Good afternoon, ladies." The stranger wore a smile as wide as a baby grand piano. He addressed all three ladies, but Jeanette noticed he never took his eyes off her. She shyly looked down at the pan of corn.

"This corn can't be as sweet as you are," he said to her.

Jeanette kept her eyes lowered and smiled.

Instead of moving along when she didn't respond, the man bent forward at the waist and turned his head to one side to make eye contact with her. "And the sunshine is no match for your beautiful smile."

Jeanette looked the stranger in his eyes and heaped some corn on his plate. "Thank you," she said.

Deacon Hughes, who was in charge of keeping the line moving, lightly tapped Tom on the arm. "Move along, young buck. Flirt on your own time."

Tom looked at Deacon Hughes and laughed. "Man, you're messing up my game."

Messing up his game? Jeanette mused. *He doesn't even know my name.* She watched as the stranger moved on to the barbeque chicken.

Stacey leaned over. "Who was that?"

Jeanette shrugged. "I don't know. Don't think I've ever seen him before."

Mary, no stranger to gossip, chimed in. "I hear he works with Deacon Hughes. Think his name is Tom something or nuther."

"Girl, you better watch out for that one," Stacey warned. "He looks slick as Miss Patty's okra."

Despite her friend's warning, Jeanette found the stranger intriguing. He looked slick alright, but not in a negative way. He was the only man at the cookout in a hat and tie. Everyone else had traded their Sunday best for casual attire, but not the stranger. His attire set him apart from the crowd.

Having completed their duties, Stacey invited Jeanette to sit with her and her sweetheart Mike, but Jeanette declined. She didn't want to be a third wheel.

She took her plate to a quiet grassy area down by the lake. She found the water reflective and welcoming and preferred sitting there.

"Well, here you are. You're a hard person to keep up with, Miss." The stranger from the serving line interrupted.

Lost in her own thoughts, Jeanette hadn't heard the stranger approach. Startled, she looked up.

"I thought you'd like a slice of melon. I had to wrestle a little boy for it. But as they say, 'To the victor—'"

"Goes the spoils," Jeanette finished and they both laughed.

"I'm Tom and your name is Jeanette," he said with a smile.

A warm feeling ran down her spine. She liked the way he said her name, and she really liked his smile. Jeanette wondered how he knew her name.

"My young friend shared that with me too," he added, as if he'd read her mind. "Cost me a whole five dollars, you know. Two for the melon and another three for your name and location."

Jeanette looked past Tom to see little Keith Smith waving at her. She smiled and waved back at the young boy.

"May I sit down?"

Jeanette nodded, and Tom joined her on the grassy knoll. They sat in silence, looking at the lake, eating their watermelon.

"I hope you don't mind me joining you. You really do look lovely." Tom turned to Jeanette and smiled.

Jeanette had worn her cornflower blue dress with the little yellow flowers. She felt pretty but not too made up, just right for a cookout. "Thank you," she said with a smile. She thought to herself, *Thank God I let Mary fix my hair today.*

Jeanette arrived at Mary's home with her hair in a ponytail, but Mary wasn't going for that. "How do you expect to get a man looking like you came in fourth at the Kentucky Derby?" She had asked Jeanette.

Laughing, Jeanette said, "Girl, we're going to work on a serving line at a cookout." But before Jeanette could blink, Mary had grabbed some bobby pins and whipped her up a new hairdo. She had also encouraged Jeanette to try on her new peach lipstick then stepped back, surveying Jeanette up and down. "There," she had said with approval, "my job is done."

"So, tell me about yourself, Jeanette." Tom's deep voice brought Jeanette out of her musing.

Jeanette found Tom to be a natural at conversing. Usually shy, she felt at ease with him and was amazed by how much she contributed to the conversation.

"One day, I'd like to have a business," Jeanette confided. "I'm not exactly sure what kind though. That's why I'm taking courses at the community college. I was working but now I'm going to school fulltime."

"A business woman," Tom mused out loud. "Nice."

They continued to talk about their past, their upbringing, and their dreams. Before she knew it, they were holding hands walking around the lake.

Jeanette was drawn to Tom and loved the time they spent together. She enjoyed preparing dinner for him after his work day ended. When they weren't enjoying a meal together, Tom took her to the movies, skating (something neither of them had done since their teens) or to visit a museum. Smitten, Jeanette thoroughly enjoyed his companionship.

Chapter 2

Tom and Jeanette were married six months after their first stroll around the lake. They set up house in a small apartment on Ludlow Street. The projects they were called.

"Baby, this is only temporary. After I get that new management position, we'll move into our own house next year," Tom promised.

As Jeanette surveyed her surroundings, she remembered her parent's offer for her and Tom to move in with them. "After all," her mother stated, "Jeanette's bedroom is spacious enough for two. You lovebirds can save on rent and put a little money away." But Tom insisted they start out fresh together, and Jeanette agreed. She'd always lived with her parents and although she was grateful for the offer, she knew it would be best for her and her husband to have a place of their own.

Jeanette wasn't used to living in a tenement with so many people crowded on top of one another. Her parents were far from rich and didn't own a home, but they rented a second-floor apartment on Seymour Avenue that was like having their own home. With access to the backyard, her family planted vegetables and flowers. In addition, they had patio furniture and a grill which was great for outdoor entertaining during the summer. She grew up in an area where everyone knew their neighbors and all the children played together.

In contrast, living in the projects was a whole different world. The halls were a benign beige color, decorated with artistic expressions of graffiti and vulgar statements. The apartment doors and the floors were a dank, dark brown. The lights were never bright enough and oftentimes, some of the bulbs were not working at all, casting a dark, depressing shadow in the halls. The elevator frequently broke down, leaving some tenants to climb twelve floors to their residence. Those who wished to do dirty deeds would knock out the lights, leaving the halls dark and foreboding. Some tenants didn't properly dispose their trash in the disposal. Instead they stuffed the garbage chute until the waste backed up. Others left their refuse in the hall, creating a buffet for vermin.

Jeanette was cordial with her neighbors. She kept company with a single mother across the hall and the elderly couple next door, but most of the people in her building appeared guarded and not very welcoming.

Despite the depressing scene outside, inside the Watson's apartment was immaculate. Jeanette not only kept the place neat and clean with an eye for details, but the apartment was beautifully decorated. Even though her furniture was all secondhand, she had a knack for finding the right pieces. She shopped at the best thrift stores and negotiated a good price on already marked down items. Some of their furniture came from the annual church bazaar and other pieces were castaways from her employers. Jeanette had live plants to keep the air clean and beautiful art adorned their walls. Next to her corner chair, was her old, black King James Bible, handed down to her from her grandmother and her mother before. The apartment was a cozy oasis for the two of them.

There was no shortage of neighbors and excitement in their community. If a party wasn't going on during the weekend, a fight certainly was. And somebody was always getting arrested. Jeanette was quiet and reserved compared to Tom's outgoing personality. Sometimes, she envied how easily he made friends. Often, Jeanette wondered if he was perhaps too good of a friend with some of the neighbors, especially those of the opposite sex.

She heard people in their complex refer to her husband as "Good Time Tom." People would laugh and say the party didn't start until Tom showed up. When he first started attending an occasional party, Jeanette hadn't been concerned. Then it escalated to a party every weekend, and sometimes the weekend didn't end until the following week. He used to invite her, but Jeanette wasn't the party type. She preferred church related activities, especially Testimony Night on Friday evening because she could pray and cry and shout her troubles away.

Had she married too soon? During their courtship, Tom attended Sunday service with her, but soon stopped after they married. The intimacy they shared began to fade as well. The red-hot sex they enjoyed in the months following their honeymoon cooled down and became more infrequent. Tom would peck her on the cheek early in the morning before leaving for work and then peck her on the cheek when he came home, if he came home at all. Many nights, he'd stumble in intoxicated and go straight to bed, leaving Jeanette to take off his clothes and tuck him under the covers.

Whenever Tom woke from his drunken stupor, Jeanette would fix him breakfast. "Tom," she'd say, "one day you're going to wake up expecting me to be in this kitchen and I'll be gone."

"What are you talking about, Jeanette?" He'd ask her.

"Tom, I'm telling you. Jesus is coming to rapture his children. He's going to take his faithful ones away and those who are not will be left behind. It'll be a terrible time—a time of weeping and gnashing of teeth. I'm warning you now, Tom, because I love you and I don't want you to suffer like that. Instead of wasting your time partying and drinking, why don't you give your life to Jesus and go to church? You ought to be evangelizing your friends and warning them so they can be saved too."

But every time Jeanette warned Tom, he laughed and called her silly and superstitious. "Honey," he'd say, giving her a hug. "That's your job. I'm just hanging out with my friends trying to blow off some steam. You know how stressful my job is."

Tom had started out as a mail sorter and then became a mail clerk. After five years, he'd become an assistant manager at the post office. He was making more money than ever with nothing to show for it. Jeanette always thought with his salary alone, they could have put a down payment on a house or, at the least, rented one. But Tom's money went as fast as it came in. He bought expensive clothes, drove a brand new 1975 Cadillac and loved to gamble. He also had a few women "on the side" to take care of. He didn't think Jeanette knew about them, but she did. When she first discovered these things about her husband, she was crushed.

She thought about leaving, but Janette had been raised to be a good Christian wife. She heard far too many sermons on marriage to know that this was against the rules. "God hates divorce," she could hear the minister's words. And lest she forget all the talk in Women's Ministry. *A woman must submit to her husband.* Besides, she didn't want to move back into her parent's home and be pitied for the rest of her life. But what if she was in a bad marriage? Should she be condemned to hell on earth because of a poor choice? Or should she leave and face hell in the afterlife?

To make ends meet, Jeanette left school and took in day work, cleaning houses for well to do families in Millburn and Livingston. She'd take two buses to work and the same two buses back home, working four days a week and sometimes on Saturdays, but she made sure of two things. One, she never missed church on Sunday and two, she always served her husband a hot dinner... Well, at least when he came home to have one. Tom was so wrapped up in himself, two whole years passed before he realized Jeanette had a job. Once he found out, he stopped paying the rent and told her if she wanted to wear the pants, she could pay the bills.

So, Jeanette did. She paid the bills and put money away in her savings account. Tom never asked Jeanette what she did with her earnings, and she never told him.

Jeanette worked hard to save money. Week after week, she cleaned houses and took in sewing on the side. A bridal gown here. A sweet sixteen dress there. Prom season was lucrative, but it was the pastor's wife who kept her busy. The first lady liked how Jeanette sewed. "Your suits make me look like I stepped off the cover of *Ebony Magazine*," she told Jeanette. Jeanette was grateful for her business and worked like a woman on a mission. Over time, she was able to put away quite a little nest egg.

Chapter 3

It seemed to Tom that Jeanette was always nagging him about going to church. He knew when he was chasing her skirt that she was a church girl. He'd wanted a church girl, someone not so wise to the ways of the world. A woman who would be submissive and stay off his back. He liked being able to come and go as he pleased — to work, to his favorite bar, home for a hot meal and when he felt like it, a little belly rub with his wife. He especially enjoyed visiting his main squeeze on the side for a little bit of sweetness before stumbling home to fall into bed. But Jeanette was getting on his nerves with this church thing. He always said no and made excuses as to why he couldn't attend, but there really wasn't any need to pretend he was interested in church now that she'd married him.

Tom settled on the couch and opened the newspaper to the sports section when she started in on him. "Tom, you're going to look for me one day and I'll be gone. Jesus is coming back for his children, and everybody else will be left behind. Yes, sir. I love you, Tom, but when my Lord comes, I can't take you with me. All those people you keep company with, you'd better tell them to get their house in order. Um-hmm, and don't forget to warn your lady friends too."

"Lady friends? What in the world are you talking about, woman? Did you forget that I'm a married man? I don't have no lady friends."

His wife's cool demeanor unnerved him. This was more than her usual cerebral behavior. Tom slid down to the other end of the couch and faced Jeanette. He leaned over and rubbed her thigh. "Honey, don't worry yourself imagining things." His wife's eyes looked cold and distant. *I thought they said Christian women were meek.*

He opened his mouth to speak, but Jeanette interjected. "I'm not going to argue with you, Tom, but I'm nobody's fool. You've been at it for a long time, and you need to be ashamed of yourself. That's all I have to say, but you remember this, we all have to answer for our sins. Jesus is coming, Tom. You'll look for me one day and I'll be gone."

Tom didn't know what to say. Jeanette rose from her chair, walked into their bedroom and closed the door. He knew he should probably go after her and try to smooth things over, but her words pierced him like cold, damp weather penetrating an old person's bones. They sounded ominous. He sat there stunned. Was his wife prescient? He shivered to shake off the feeling. *How did she know?* He'd been so careful, at least he thought he had. *Does she know about Pauline, Bonnie, and my new squeeze, Candy? She is creeping me out with how calm she is. Should I be worried?*

Tom stood and paced the room, resolving inwardly not to go out so much anymore "Yeah," Tom said to himself as he hid the sharp knives. *I definitely think I should stay home a little bit more.*

For the next month, Tom went to work and came straight home. He didn't stop at the bar or party on the weekends and there were no chicks on the side. Although he didn't go to church, he displayed model behavior. He took Jeanette out a few times, bowling and to the movies. He even helped around the house. They even sat outside, from time to time, and talked. He could tell Jeanette was much happier and strangely, so was he.

One beautiful day, the best they had experienced in a long time, Tom packed a lunch and took Jeanette to the park. He parked the car, and they walked hand in hand to the clearing.

"Oh, Tom!" Jeanette laid her head on his shoulder. "You remembered. This is our place." They were at the very spot where they shared melon all those years ago.

Together, they spread a blanket on the grass and sat down to eat lunch. Tom tuned the portable radio to their favorite station, WNJR and began singing along with the tune, *It only takes a minute to fall in love.* "This song reminds me of us, Jenny. It only took a minute for me." He closed his eyes, reminiscing. "Girl, I saw you in that blue dress, mmm, it hugged you in all the right places. You were so shy back then and I loved it."

"Yea, I fell for you too, Tom. You were so handsome and so sure of yourself. You seemed to have a confidence that I'd never seen in another man."

"Dance with me," Tom stood and held out his hand.

"Here?"

"Yes, here, woman. Come on, dance with your man."

"You sure, brother? Cause you know I got moves."

Tom let out a deep laugh that seemed to come from way down in his toes. Jeanette couldn't keep time to fast songs. Fortunately for her, the song ended, and they found themselves in a sweet embrace swaying to Natalie Cole's *Inseparable.*

"Thomas Watson," Jeanette said in a low sultry voice, "I do believe you are courting me." Tom closed his eyes and smiled. Hearing his name like that resounded sweetly in his ear. Suddenly he had feelings for Jeanette that sent his mind soaring. Was he feeling a rebirth of love or was he loving her for the first time? They hugged and kissed like teenagers, and back at home, they made love passionately as if for the first time.

Tom lay with Jeanette nestled under his arm, her head resting on his chest. "I love you. You've been a good wife. I'm sorry for everything I've put you through. Please forgive me."

"I already have, Tom. I'm glad we're starting over."

Tom nodded in agreement. "I have a surprise for you."

Jeanette rolled on her side, supporting herself on her elbow so she could see his face. "Really? You know how I love surprises."

"Well, I've decided to go to church with you tomorrow."

Jeanette sprung up, jumping up and down on the bed like a five-year-old child.

Jeanette

Sleep was sweet. Jeanette dreamed her and Tom were getting married again. She was dressed in a glorious white gown surrounded by her friends Stacey, Mary, and Lena. They each held glasses filled with champagne and clinked them together in a toast.

The glasses clinked and clinked and clinked.

Jeanette woke up. It wasn't champagne glasses, someone was knocking at the door. She opened her eyes to Tom leaving the bedroom, but remained in bed, quietly listening.

"Who is it?" She heard Tom ask.

Jeanette couldn't hear the reply, but she heard Tom turning the locks to open the door.

"Candy, what are you doing here?" Tom asked in a loud whisper. "I told you never come to my house."

Jeanette got out of bed and grabbed her robe. She tipped down the hall, stuffing her arms through the holes. Back against the wall, she spied around the corner. Candy looked like she belonged on "Hookers Row" with her cheap, platinum blonde Afro Wig, silver eyeshadow and lips so glossy they could be used to guide ships into the harbor at Port Newark. The woman's purple mini dress was so tight, Jeanette thought it looked like a girdle. *So, this is the infamous Candy?* She started to confront them but decided to see what her husband would do.

"Baby, it's been so long, and I've really missed you." Candy seductively rubbed her curvaceous hip with one hand and touched her bottom lip with the index finger of the other. "Why haven't you come by to see me? Don't you miss your sweet Candy?"

Jeanette rolled her eyes. *This is sickening.*

Tom covered Candy's mouth with his hand. "Shhh. Keep your voice down. I don't want you to wake up my wife."

Candy knocked his hand away. "Oh, Miss High and Mighty, Self-Righteous Sister knows what time it is. It's Candy time, baby, and I've got the flavor you like."

Tom opened the door. "Here, wait for me in the hall. I'll be right there."

Jeanette hurried back to bed and pulled the covers over her, pretending to be asleep. Through slit eyes, she watched Tom tiptoe into the bedroom. Sensing he would turn to look at her, she shut her eyes. She could hear him moving around the room. She dared to peer through slit eyes again and watched him dress. He grabbed his wallet and keys and slipped quietly out the door. Jeanette heard the apartment door close and sat up in bed. She threw her pillow across the room as tears flooded her eyes. *How could I have been such a fool? How could I actually believe he really loved me? He was just pretending to have changed. How many nights has he snuck out while I was sleeping? All the praying and love making didn't change a thing.*

Her mind was a battlefield. "This is it," Jeanette said aloud. "I know exactly what to do."

Chapter 4

One Week Later

That night in the hallway outside of his apartment, Tom intended to tell Candy their relationship was over. He and his wife were together and that's the way it was going to be. But Candy had other plans. She suggested they go to her home instead of having their discussion in a public place. Not wanting his business in the streets, Tom agreed. Candy poured him a drink and one drink led to another. Having been off the wagon for a month, intoxication came quickly and one day flowed into the next. Seven days had passed since he'd seen Jeanette, but it felt more like seven years.

Tom went to work hungover. Again.

He had called in sick two straight days after drinking most of the week. He only showed up at the office today because it was payday. But who would miss the smell of alcohol seeping from his pores? It smelled bad even to him. He wondered how long before his boss, Joe Giddeon, took notice and fired him.

Joe, a tall thin man whose pale skin always reminded Tom of a sorrowful mortician, stood in the doorway. Tom imagined him dressed in black performing a eulogy. *Here lies the remains of Thomas Watson.* Tom would have laughed, but to do so would only add more pain to his already aching head. Tom sat in his office chair, feeling small like a child. He hoped Joe would have pity on him and leave him alone, but there was no pity to be had. He told Tom not to return to the office unless he was sober and suspended him for two weeks without pay.

Tom packed up his belongings and headed home. *Home? Where is home?* He couldn't go back to Jeanette after leaving the way he did. Was Candy's apartment home now? *Is she what I really want?*

Tom wandered around for most of the day until he ended up back at Candy's place. Before he could knock, she opened the door. "Baby, you don't look so good, but I know what will make you feel better. Let's go out."

The scene was set as soon as they stepped through the door of the club. The blue light made everyone appear dream-like. The waitresses' outfits glowed in the dark like popular velvet posters. The waitress smiled and handed them a drink. "First drink is on the house."

Tom drank fast and ordered another.

Candy laughed and chided him. "Slow down, cowboy. You want to be around for the whole rodeo."

And a rodeo it was. All his friends seemed to be there, Curtis, Bill and Pete. Everybody was in a celebratory mood. It was Friday and for most, it was payday. There was a card game going on in one room and a game of craps being played in a secret room out back.

Curtis said, "Let's see if the dice are hot tonight."

He, Tom and Candy joined the group shooting dice. Tom lost a few games, but eventually doubled what was in his wallet. He had so much money it looked like his wallet was going to burst.

Candy couldn't contain her excitement. "Daddy, let your Candy Girl hold some of that before you lose it." He gave her five-hundred dollars, which she quickly slipped into her bra. When he'd had his fill, they left the dice game and went into the main room to dance.

The room seemed darker than usual. The music was louder than usual, and the drinks appeared to be stronger than usual. Scantily dressed women surrounded him, dancing, brushing against him. Tom felt claustrophobic. The lights changed from blue to amber to red. He felt a bit dizzy and took a seat at the nearest booth.

Candy stood over him in her form-fitting crimson dress. "What's wrong, baby?" She sat on his lap and opened her purse.

"I'm feeling a little light headed, that's all."

She retrieved a breath mint from her bag and popped it in her mouth. "You mean after all this time, you can't hold your liquor, Daddy?" She kissed him with her blood red lips. "That's okay. Let Candy take care of you."

There were whispered promises of sexual exploration, but Tom's mind wasn't on Candy. Why had he agreed to come to this place? Why didn't he just go back to Jeanette?

"Here, baby, take another sip. You'll feel better." Candy held the glass to his mouth and he drank more. "There now. That's it, baby. Drink all your milk." She set the glass on the table and laughed, kissing him again. While rubbing his chest, she deftly removed his wallet from his breast pocket, placed it in her open purse and snapped it closed. Without missing a beat, Candy continued to kiss him and rub the back of his neck.

The thumping music grew louder, and Tom pulled away from her embrace. He looked at all the people and suddenly their faces appeared to become distorted and hideous.

"Get Off Me!" Tom yelled.

Fearing she'd been found out, Candy jumped up. "What's the matter, baby?"

"Get away from me!" Tom yelled. "Get away from me!" He stood too fast and the blood rushed to his head. Then there was darkness.

Tom woke up on the floor. Broken glass, furniture and bodies were strewn all over the room. He couldn't believe the scene. Still shaken, he stood and saw others staggering to their feet. He looked down to see Candy trying to stand. Shards of glass were embedded in her hair, twinkling like eerie Christmas lights. She was bleeding quite a bit from the forehead, crying and calling out his name.

Tom found a napkin and wiped the glass off a nearby chair. He helped Candy off the floor and sat her on the chair, then turned and walked away. He could hear her calling his name, but her voice sounded like it was in a vacuum. As if moving in slow motion, stepping over people and glass he made his way to the door.

There was complete mayhem in the streets. Sirens from police cars, fire trucks and ambulances assaulted his ears. Broken glass and injured people were everywhere. Traffic was at a total standstill due to vehicle accidents. Fires burned, and smoke filled the air. He looked up and the sun was blood red. Tom ripped the lining from his jacket to cover his nose and mouth. He ran toward home — his and Jeanette's home. He hurried as fast as he could, stopping only to catch his breath.

Even though his mouth and nose were masked, he still coughed. He walked then picked up the pace again, until finally he arrived at home. He surveyed the apartment complex. Most of the windows were okay, though some had been blown out and a few others had cracks in them. It seemed like all the residents were outside talking. But Tom, still in shock, could not make out a word they were saying.

He entered his apartment. "Jeanette! Jeanette! Jenny! Jenny! Jenny, where are you?" He searched the living room, bedroom, bathroom and then the kitchen. Exasperated, he turned to see a handwritten note taped to the refrigerator.

Dear Tom,
I told you one day I'll be gone. I'll miss you.
Love,
J.

Tom let out a blood curdling scream, crying and moaning until he felt nauseous. He hurried to the toilet and vomited, heaving incessantly until he almost passed out again. He flung open the apartment door and ran into the hallway. Tom banged on his neighbor's door until the lady opened it. "Where's Jenny?" He asked frantically. Before the lady could answer, Tom bolted down the stairs screaming her name.

He asked everyone he saw, "Where's Jenny?" But no one knew. Tom looked up at the red sky, his eyes big as saucers. He took a deep breath and yelled, "Repent. Repent! It's the rapture! Jesus is here! Jesus is here!"

Frantically running down the street, Tom told every person he saw. "It's the rapture." He resembled a fire and brimstone preacher with his index finger shaking back and forth, rising above his head. Pointing, he bellowed. "Look! The sky is red. Jesus is here! Repent!" He told the children. He told the firemen. He told the young and the old. He told everybody. Still running down the street, he thought to himself, *I've got to get to the church.*

Inside Christian Missionary Church, the pews were filled with injured people, bleeding and moaning. Ambulance workers bandaged up the wounded. Others were draped in Red Cross blankets, sipping hot soup. He ran to the pulpit. "Jesus has come on a cloud," Tom declared. "The sounding trumpet shook the earth, and believers have been raptured away. All of us were left behind because we didn't believe. Let's all call on Jesus right now. Let's repent and ask his forgiveness and mercy. Join me now! Right now! Give your life to Jesus."

Some people came forward. Others began to pray, while others shouted, "Forgive us, Jesus!"

Pastor Clemmons came forward and patted Tom on the back to console him. "Tom. Brother Tom, it's okay."

Tom was confused. "Pastor, what are you doing here? Of all the people who have been raptured, you should be gone. Why are you still here?"

The pastor looked at Tom. "I've been waiting for you."

Tom was overwhelmed. "Y-you waited for me?" He fell into the pastor's arms and wept.

A police officer walked up, but Pastor Clemmons held his hand up to stop him. "I know this man. I'll take care of him myself." He took Tom into his office and instructed him to lie down on the sofa, assuring him that he'd be alright.

In a hoarse voice, Tom asked, "Where's my Jenny?"

The pastor replied. "Jeanette is gone."

Once more, Tom began to weep, calling her name over and over until he fell asleep. Tom slept through the night and late into the afternoon of the following day. He awoke to a bundle of clean clothes and a note instructing him to utilize the private bathroom to clean himself up.

Although Tom was hungover and his head was pounding, the wash up and shave refreshed him. He dressed and went in search of the pastor, finding him in his office.

Pastor Clemmons greeted him. "I suggest you eat the saltines first then sip on the ginger ale." The pastor handed him two aspirin. "I learned that tip from my wife when she had morning sickness."

Tom ate the crackers and took a few sips of soda before swallowing the aspirin.

The pastor offered him a cup of chicken broth and Tom accepted.

"Pastor, what am I going to do without my Jenny?" He sipped the warm soup.

"I don't know, Tom. What do you plan to do? You can't continue going through life the way you have. It's destructive and God has given you so much. He spared your life. You have a loving wife and a good job, but you go around throwing it all away on parties and fast women. Is that what you want?"

Tom looked sorrowful. "No, I want to be with Jeanette. She always warned me to repent, but I would laugh. I want to give my life to Jesus. I want to change, and I want to be with my wife."

"That's good, Tom," The pastor nodded, "but you have some work to do. First things first, you need to get sober and stay sober. There is an Alcoholics Anonymous group that meets here twice a week. They'd be glad to welcome you."

The pastor leaned forward and looked at Tom. They were practically, nose to nose. "You were mumbling about your job in your sleep. You said your manager didn't fire you?"

"I was?" Tom hung his head. "He suspended me without pay for two weeks and told me not to return to work until I was sober."

"Brother, you are indeed a blessed man. Most people would have fired you. God is good." The pastor lifted his hands in praise. "Tom, my wife and I would like to offer you a place with us for a while until you are stronger. Is that okay?"

Tom nodded, undone by the pastor's hospitable offer. He knew he didn't want to stay in Candy's apartment anymore, but he wasn't sure he could return to him and Jeanette's home without her being there.

"Good," Pastor Clemons said, patting him on the back, "because I've already moved your clothes into our extra bedroom."

After reassuring Tom the rapture didn't happen, Pastor Clemmons explained that the chemical plant on Frelinghuysen Avenue had a powerful explosion. It had impacted all of the community within a three-mile radius of the plant. Homes and businesses were destroyed. Others experienced broken windows and blown out doors. The bar Tom had been in at the time was pretty much decimated.

"And the red sky?" Tom asked.

"News reports say that was due to the smoke in the atmosphere. We have that sometimes in the summer during sunset, but this was strictly due to the explosion," the pastor explained.

Tom looked embarrassed. "So if Jeanette hasn't been raptured, where is my wife? You said she was gone."

"Well, Tom," Pastor Clemmons said, "Jeanette has been counseling with my wife and me. She told us about everything that's happened, the drinking, gambling and the infidelity." The pastor reached into his pocket and pulled out an envelope. "She asked me to give you this. It will explain everything." The pastor handed Tom the letter and left the study to allow him some privacy.

Dear Tom,

By now you know I've left you. I was so in love with you and I was willing to go on living with you. But after last week, when you left with that woman, I knew I had to get out of this relationship. I used to say I loved three things: God, you and my church. But now I've learned to love my God with all my heart, soul and might. And, to love ME. Everybody and everything else will have to get in line to earn their way into my heart.

I told you, one day I'd leave. Well, I have. As you can see, I've moved my furniture and other belongings. I also took care to bring along your antique clock and your mother's ring because I didn't want to leave them for someone to steal. So if you'd like, you can pick them up. I live at 225 Clinton Place, and I'll be home tomorrow night at 6:30.

J.

Chapter 5

Tom arrived at 6:30 sharp. He walked up the steps of the big old house, admiring the wraparound porch. He approached the door, noticing the nameplate read J. Watson, and rang the bell.

Jeanette peeked out the curtain and opened the door, welcoming him in.

"Wow! This place is huge." Tom said looking around. From the foyer, he could see her living room, sitting room, and down the hall into the dining area. "How can you afford all this?"

"Well, hello to you too, Tom. And if you must know, I saved every dollar I could. I purchased only what was necessary and made my clothes or bought them secondhand. You already know I didn't have to spend much money on food since most of the time I shopped for *one*."

He looked at her shamefully, but Jeanette plowed on.

"And, my employers were very kind to me. They insisted I help myself to anything I wanted to eat, so that really helped me save."

"I'm really proud of you, Jenny, and I'm sorry for not giving you a proper greeting. It's just... Well... You can't possibly afford this place. Can you? It has to be expensive."

For the first time in their marriage, Jeanette raised her voice. "Expensive, Tom? Expensive? You were not worried about me and my expenses when you were out on the town with your so-called friends. You go out and do whatever you want for weeks at a time caring less about what happens to me so please don't pretend to care now." She took a deep breath, she hadn't meant to get upset. "This house belongs to First Lady Clemons, Tom. She inherited it from an aunt, and she's renting it to me at a considerable discount. My sewing business is really picking up. I have at least a dozen first ladies as clients and a few out of state. I plan to turn the sitting room into a sewing room and studio. By the new year, I'll be able to cut back on cleaning houses to just one or two days a week and then I can devote most of my time to sewing." Smugly, she added, "All in all, I'm doing just fine on my own."

Tom hung his head. When he looked at her, he had tears in his eyes. "Jenny, I'm sorry. I'm sorry for hurting you like this. I've been selfish, thinking only of myself and my own needs." He reached out for her hand. "I've made a lot of mistakes, but I want to make it up to you. Please, Jenny. I want us to start over again. Please let me make it up to you."

"Tom, there is nothing to make up. What we had is gone and I'm not about living in the past. The past is not my address anymore, and it's not where I live. God is working in my present and my future and if you want to live there with me, you've got a lot of work to do. We've got a lot of work to do."

* * *

One year later, Jeanette sat in the front pew next to the first lady and pastor. The sanctuary was packed elbow to elbow with both regular parishioners and guests. Others sat in the overflow room. Since the chemical plant accident, church attendance had exploded.

All eyes were on the guest speaker. Jeanette held newborn baby Tommy in her arms and surveyed the room. Many people from her old building were there. Pete, Curtis, and to her surprise, Joe Giddeon, sat behind her.

There was a hush as the speaker stepped up to the podium. "Good morning, everyone. My name is Thomas Watson, and today, I'd like to share my testimony with you." Tom wiped his brow and smiled his classic smile, wide as a baby grand piano. "There was a time when I looked for my wife and she was long gone. But love called my name and offered me a new start."

About the Author

Talk Show Host, Speaker, Author, Life Coach and "Daughter of The King." Leslie K. Howard is a woman who "Lives Life On Purpose, With Purpose." Leslie's books include *Sisters with S.A.S.S. (Saved Anointed Smart Successful Women of God)* and *Love Letters from God: Psalm 23*. She also hosts Sister Circle Girlfriends Getaway Weekend, a destination conference for women and their best friends. Leslie and her husband, former Pastor Franklin K. Howard, have two adult children and three beautiful grandchildren.

Spring Blues
Annie Johnson

Chapter One

I, Spring Vaughn, owner of Vaughn Physical Therapy Association, finally looked up from my freshly, cleaned desk. All paperwork had been officially filed away digitally on my computer. Being a health nut who took particular care of my six-foot, curvy frame, I could tell it was time to enjoy the salad I'd made for lunch. I very seldom ate in the break room, but I had to get away from my office. The walls were closing in on me. My heels clicked as I walked on the marble floor towards the break room. At some point, my exhaustion started to climb up my legs and I found myself scooting and shuffling my feet lazily by the time I reached the break room door.

Before entering, I looked around the large cold room to see who was in there. Not many were in the room, mostly men watching a basketball game. They pumped fists and shouted sports lingo. I found a seat near the entrance, made myself comfortable and tore into the delicious salad like a mad woman.

I looked up at the television as the referee blew his whistle and called a foul. I let out a sigh, rolled my eyes. The game suddenly reminded me of my cheating, lying, control freak ex-boyfriend, Clarence Montgomery. *Ugh!*

I picked up my salad bowl and returned to my office, slumping into my desk chair. Clarence was six feet five inches tall with a mellow yellow skin complexion and curly hair, and he could beat everyone on the basketball court.

The talented creep.

The tall lean basketball playing machine as he was often described in the school newspaper back in the day was my first love. He was also the man that broke my heart leaving me to swear off dating athletes.

The captain of the basketball team where I attended college. I was devastated after catching him red-handed with his pants down. *The low-down punk!*

Memories of him cheating on me flooded my mind. I remembered walking into his dorm room that rainy afternoon, opening the door to his pants pulled down around his shoes.

My mouth flew wide open, "Clarence! What? How could you? You low down dirty dog."

He had tried to pull his pants up in a hurry. "Spring, wait. It's not what you think. I can explain!"

But I slammed the door hard and took off running back to my dorm room. I fell across my bed sobbing uncontrollably as my body shook.

From that day on, I avoided Clarence like the plague. If I saw him coming toward me, I went in the opposite direction. I would not return any of his calls and called campus security every time he knocked on my door. He was so livid when I called security, but I didn't care. He deserved it.

Years later, my eyes still watered at the memory of his backside and the pain and heartbreak. I was crushed for life, or so I thought. To this day, I do not know what I would have done if it were not for my best friend and sorority sister, Rolonda Flowers, Esq. She was my rock. She stood by me and remained supportive.

The telephone rang shaking me out of my commiserating. I looked at the caller ID and smiled, Rolonda. I barely said hello before Rolonda started rambling.

"Girl, slow down so I can understand what you're saying." I said.

She was clearly distressed. And as she continued, my smile drooped.

I sat up in my desk chair. "Are you kidding me? Of course, Rolonda, he's your cousin. My firm will gladly take DeMarco on as a patient. I have the perfect physical therapist in mind. Venezuela is the best. I will get her to work with the team to ensure that DeMarco gets the best care and has a speedy recovery. We will have him back on the football field in no time."

"I was so nervous," Rolonda said.

"I imagine you were."

I scribbled a note on a pad and buzzed my receptionist. When she entered, I put my finger up to my mouth, so she would not say anything, and then handed her the note. She nodded.

"Rolonda, I am leaving my office in a little while. Why don't I go by the hospital and check on DeMarco? I can talk to the doctor while I'm there."

"Thanks, Spring, I knew I could count on you. I'll call him and let him know you're coming. I love my cousin and want the best for him." She let out a big sigh. "I am exhausted. I was at the hospital all night with DeMarco's parents and my parents. We tried to get DeMarco's parents to go home and get some rest, but they wouldn't listen. They refuse to leave his side, and they're just sitting there looking defeated with their shoulders slumped, staring at DeMarco. It's painful to watch. I came home to get some sleep and regroup before I head back to the hospital this evening."

There was clipped knock at my door and my receptionist entered. She laid the patient release forms I needed to take to the hospital on my desk. We would need DeMarco's signature before I could speak with his physician and obtain his x-rays.

"I do understand what his parents are going through," I attempted to console my friend. "He's their child and they are concerned about the seriousness of his injuries. Maybe when you return later this evening, they will listen to you and go home. You get some rest, soror. I will talk to you later."

I hung up the phone, overwhelmed with empathy for DeMarco and his family. *He must be terrified. I hope it wasn't a career ending injury.*

I didn't know a whole lot about football, but I closed my office door and turned my TV to ESPN just in time to catch the replay of the hit. I watched DeMarco Blues go down on the field and grabbed my chest. "Ouch. DeMarco got hit hard."

I couldn't erase what happened to DeMarco, but my company could help him heal.

Chapter Two

I grabbed my keys and drove the short distance to the hospital. DeMarco was resting when I entered his hospital room. My heart skipped a beat watching him lying there. I looked around the room at the beeping monitors and nodded hello to the nurses who were busy adjusting the monitors in the room. I waited patiently as they took care of DeMarco. He opened his eyes, and I jumped at the opportunity to get the release papers signed.

"Hello, DeMarco."

"You must be Spring. Rolonda said you would be stopping by."

I nodded. "I won't stay long, but I needed to get your signature on these release forms so we can coordinate with your doctor for your physical therapy. I'd like to have your x-rays sent over to my office as soon as possible."

DeMarco closed his eyes and sighed. "Of course, let me sign the release paper so that will be taken care of."

I laid the papers as close as possible in hopes of causing the least amount of distress.

DeMarco beamed at me, before signing the papers. "By the way, you are gorgeous."

Flustered, I laughed nervously. "They must have you on some really strong pain medication, but thank you. I appreciate the compliment, DeMarco."

I knew Rolonda's cousin was quite handsome, but this was the first time I had seen him in person, and he was even more handsome in person. DeMarco's compliment had me doing a double take before I left his hospital room. I'd read a few magazine articles about DeMarco Blues and his various women. Another cheating athlete, I assumed. Although, Rolonda said the stories were not true. She always told me not to believe everything I read.

I knew I wanted my top therapist, Venezuela to work with DeMarco on his recovery. As soon as I arrived home, I went to my office and dialed her phone number.

"Hi, Venezuela, I have a high-profile client I need you to take on. Pro football player, DeMarco Blues."

"I know who he is," Venezuela said, sounding horrible. She erupted into a coughing spasm and then sneezed so loud, I moved the phone away from my ear. "Ugh, excuse me. I watch him play ball all the time."

"Oh girl, you sound terrible!"

"I know. I have the flu."

"Oh, Venezuela, I had no idea. Don't worry about DeMarco. You focus on getting well yourself."

"I can add him to my caseload when I come back. I would love to work with DeMarco."

"I know from experience you are a strong warrior type woman and would kick the flu's rump and come back to work soon. But please, don't worry about work, concentrate on getting better. I'll get someone to take over your patients until you return, and we'll talk soon. Take care of yourself."

Genuinely concerned with Venezuela's health, I looked over her caseload to figure out how I could divide her patients among the remaining therapists.

"Oh no!" I smacked my lips. "I'm going to have to treat DeMarco myself." I plopped DeMarco's file in my open case tray. I knew I could not refer him to another company, Rolonda would have a fit.

I leaned back in my office chair, crossed my legs and looked out of the window.

Business is business.

Chapter Three

A week later, DeMarco had his first appointment. I was at the door to greet him when he arrived with one of my winning smiles. "Hi, DeMarco, your therapist is sick with the flu. Until she recovers, I will be your therapist."

DeMarco looked me up and down. I assumed by the twinkle in his eye that he liked what he saw. "I was hoping you would be my therapist," he said.

I stepped back a few inches. "Temporarily, until your therapist returns from sick leave." I wanted to stop whatever he was thinking in its tracks. I, Spring Vaughn, did not date athletes. "Follow me," I said.

We entered the therapy room, and I closed the door behind us as my attendant helped DeMarco lay on the table.

While DeMarco adjusted his position on the table, I examined his x-ray. Before I turned to address him, I reviewed the report once more. He was my best friend's cousin so I wanted him to get extra care.

DeMarco interrupted. "Spring, I really appreciate you taking care of me personally. The hit happened so fast." He pumped his arms to demonstrate. "I was running to make a touchdown, and before I knew it, I was down on the field in excruciating pain."

I walked over and smiled. "I imagine you were devastated, but I promise, everything is going to be okay." I reached for his ankle. "Is it tender when I touch you right here?"

"Ouch! Be careful, girl." Demarco chuckled.

I really didn't need this silliness and gave him a stern look. "Stop faking before I hurt your other leg."

DeMarco's brown eyes grew wide, and his mesmerizing grin appeared. "Okay, okay. And yes, my ankle is tender."

I continued my assessment and made notes on his chart.

"Okay, DeMarco, I think we're done for today. I'll stop by your house on Wednesday to teach you some mild exercises and perform a heat treatment."

"I will be delighted to see you," he winked.

My cheeks grew warm from his gesture. "You are such a flirt. Don't get any ideas. I'll be bringing an attendant with me."

Chapter Four

Wednesday morning, an attendant and I went to DeMarco's home to begin his therapy regimen. After having him complete some light exercises, I performed a heat treatment and then gave him a full body massage. Boy, did he have a strong sexy body. I closed my eyes. *My goodness, this is feeling way too good.*

I shook my head, mentally scolding myself for being unprofessional. *Girl, get a grip!* I made a mental note to have my attendant perform any future massages while I was treating DeMarco.

By the second week, DeMarco had made rapid improvement. He was able to put a little pressure on his ankle and could walk with one of his crutches for short periods of time. I had to slow him down from doing an excessive amount of exercise, explaining that good form was more important at this stage of his therapy to strengthen his ankle. Overall, I was proud of his progress.

When Venezuela returned to work, I delivered DeMarco's file to her so she could assess his progress and assume responsibility for his therapy. Secretly, I was happy Venezuela had returned. I noticed that my heart beat faster whenever DeMarco was present, and the smoldering gaze in his brown eyes caused me great difficulty with keeping my composure when I looked at him. I often found myself looking away quickly.

I was clearly more interested in DeMarco the man than DeMarco the physical therapy patient. Not that his care had suffered, but my feelings toward him had certainly grown and that was dangerous. I, Spring Vaughn, did not date athletes.

Chapter Five

DeMarco and I talked frequently on the phone after Venezuela took over his therapy. No longer concerned with maintaining professional boundaries, we began to share some deep conversations. So, I shouldn't have been surprised when he asked, "How is your love life, Spring?"

"Love life? What love life?" I smacked my lips. "My controlling, crazy ex messed that up when I busted his behind cheating red handed."

Demarco waited a beat before he responded. "I am sorry to hear that, Spring. You did not deserve that. But now I understand why you are kind of standoffish."

"Standoffish? I guess you're right, DeMarco. But, I'm not trying to go through that again."

My words hung in the space between us until DeMarco said, "Honey, you can't stop living because of what your ex did. Trust me. Let me show you how you should be treated. I would never hurt you, Spring. No one is perfect. No relationship is perfect. But with me, one thing you will never have to worry about is cheating. I am a one woman at a time man, and the one woman I want is you."

I blew out a loud breath.

"I hear you blowing," DeMarco said. "But, I am not giving up, so you might as well trust me. You are my cousin's bestie and I would not want to feel her wrath should I treat you as less than the queen you are. Release the past. Embrace the future. Your ex has moved on. He's going on with his life while you're stuck in the past. Don't let him win!"

I, Spring Vaughn, did not date athletes. Could I do this? Trust again. Love again.

Chapter Six

When the telephone rang, I snatched it up thinking it was DeMarco.

"Hello."

"Hi, lady."

This was not the voice I wanted to hear.

"What do you want, Clarence? How did you get my number and why are you calling me?"

"Is that the way you answer the telephone?"

I slammed the phone down so hard I almost broke it. *Why was Clarence Montgomery calling me? Punk butt!* His voice irked me worse than someone scraping their fingers on a chalkboard.

I stomped back to the couch where I was busy doing nothing. An hour later I heard a knock on my door. I grabbed my wallet thinking it was the pizza delivery man and snatched open the door, grinning in anticipation. My smile turned into a frown, and my eyes bucked larger than a saucer.

"Let me explain, Spring." Clarence said.

I slammed the door in his face.

The sheer gall of this man coming to my house. How does he even know where I live?

"Heifer." Clarence yelled through my closed door.

Distressed, I went back to my comfortable position on the couch and called Rolonda. I knew she would let me vent my frustrations.

A few days later, I sat in my office reading the newspaper and stumbled upon an article in the entertainment section. The headline read, "Therapist cures the Blues." The article featured a grainy picture of DeMarco and I with the writer speculating, "Famed football player DeMarco Blues has been spotted out and about smiling, laughing, and holding hands with physical therapist Spring Vaughn. Could this be serious?"

I looked at the date on the article and wondered if perhaps this was why Clarence had crawled out of his hole after all this time. *Creep!*

I sat the paper down and picked up a client's x-ray to review. My telephone rang. This time I made sure to check the caller ID. I smiled. *DeMarco.*

"Hey, what's happening?" I asked.

"Not much, lady. How are you? Is there something you want to tell me?" DeMarco sounded pissed, but I wasn't sure why.

"No, not that I know of. What's up? You sound distressed."

"I am. Do you want to tell me about a visitor you had recently?"

Oh no! How did he know?

"You mean Clarence, my ex? He came to my house, but I handled it. You have nothing to worry about. I do not want that monster. You know how much pain he caused me. I'm sure the only reason he surfaced is because he saw the newspaper article about us."

"Well, if he shows up at your house again, let me know and I will be there or my security will be there. I gotta go, I need to cool off."

"DeMarco, wait! Don't hang up."

"I'll call you later, babe."

Chapter Seven

My sorority sister Rolonda owned homes in Los Angeles and Las Vegas, and we were both long overdue for a vacation. Rolonda wanted to spend some time at her home in the city of lights and invited me to go with her. I thought about it for a quick minute and decided to take my friend up on her offer to spend a few days in sunny Las Vegas. I needed to get away from work and have some fun.

Rolonda's home in Vegas was just the spot. There was always something new going on in Vegas. Never a dull moment in this town. Pool parties, slot machines, a few shows and a good dose of some unhealthy food was just what I needed.

Shortly after we arrived at Rolonda's home in Vegas, the doorbell rang, and she asked me to answer the door. I opened the door and put my hand over my mouth in shock. DeMarco and his best friend Rusty stood there laughing.

"Wow, Rolonda didn't tell me you guys would be joining us." I folded my arms and gazed into DeMarco's sexy brown eyes. "And why didn't you mention you were coming when I talked to you on the phone? What a surprise."

"A pleasant surprise, I hope. I asked her not to tell you." DeMarco leaned in toward my ear. "Now, close your mouth."

I laughed as he and Rusty walked past me into Rolonda's huge house. When I turned and saw the grin on my friend's face, I shook my head at her. *Always matchmaking.*

I was in Vegas for a good time not a mate. We went to a dance club the first night, and the following night, we went to some of the casinos on the strip. We didn't stay too long because no one wanted DeMarco to hurt his leg.

One night while in Vegas, Rolonda threw a pool party and invited some of our college friends we hadn't seen in a while.

I watched DeMarco's eyes follow me as I strutted over to the pool area in my bikini. I knew my body was tight with as much time as I spent in the gym. Still, I was feeling a little self-conscious knowing DeMarco was checking me out. I grabbed my wrap and covered up, so all my goodies wouldn't be showing.

DeMarco was signing autographs in the middle of the party. I figured this came with the price of fame and he was used to it. For a moment, I felt jealous of the women that surrounded DeMarco. I turned away, determined to enjoy the party. Instead of focusing on the crowd around DeMarco, I helped myself to a few glasses of Cabernet Sauvignon.

A few of our sorority sisters began to do some old step moves from our college days, and I joined in. At some point, I looked up and saw DeMarco watching me as I danced. I had to admit, it felt good to have his attention.

The next night, Rolonda and I worked together on the meal. Both of us were great cooks and enjoyed cooking, but it wasn't something either of us got to do very often. I went old school to show off my culinary skills preparing ham, collard greens, macaroni and cheese, candied sweet potatoes and an old fashion coconut cake for dessert.

DeMarco nodded his head while he ate. Later, he rubbed his tummy. "Girl, you sure can cook."

His comment brought a big grin to my face. Why do I still have reservations about this man?

I wanted to protect my heart, and he was an athlete. I couldn't take another heartbreak. Was I finally admitting to myself that I was afraid? I immersed myself in work to keep from having a social life, but I had only grown lonely in the process.

I liked DeMarco a lot. So why was I constantly resisting his advances? Would I lose him if I continued? *What's a girl to do?*

Our last night in Vegas, DeMarco's friend invited us all aboard his yacht for a late-night dinner party. This was my first time on a yacht, and I sat next to DeMarco.

I could get use to this type of living.

Again, fans walked up to DeMarco for autographs. I was impressed with the way he treated his fans. I still wondered what the ladies with the short tight dresses wanted besides an autograph.

He was very polite and gracious, peering over at me. "Sorry about this, Spring."

I shot him a winning smile. "No problem. I know this comes with fame."

Despite the attention from his fans, I enjoyed the conversation we had during dinner. I found myself relaxing and enjoying DeMarco's company.

This I could get used to.

When we returned to the vacation house, DeMarco kissed me on the lips and retired to his room for the night. This was the first time Rolonda had seen us in an intimate exchange, and she was grinning from ear to ear. I rolled my eyes at her, but found myself smiling as I touched my lips. I practically floated to my room. I packed for the trip home and later drifted to sleep thinking about DeMarco.

The party is over.

Although I enjoyed the kiss, I forced my thoughts away, vowing inwardly to remain cautious.

Chapter Eight

A few weeks after our Vegas trip, I leaned back in my office chair, quite disturbed about DeMarco's reluctance to return to the field. DeMarco was eleven weeks in to a four to twelve-week recovery period, and I was becoming convinced DeMarco was afraid to return to playing football despite his healing progress. He often had a faraway look when I mentioned his return to the game.

It made no sense to keep taking his money when he was ready to return to the game. I assumed the hit had more of an effect on him than he wanted to admit. Since we were having dinner at my house, I determined it would be a great time to ask him.

Demarco arrived and settled himself on my couch.

"DeMarco, how is your ankle feeling today?"

"It still feels a little sore." He said, massaging his ankle.

I sighed. "Are you afraid to get back on the football field?"

"Of course not." He lifted his eyebrow. "What kind of ridiculous question is that? You think I am a punk or something?"

Not at all intimidated by the frustration in his tone, I looked him in the eye before speaking in a soothing, sympathetic manner. "Think about what I am saying, DeMarco. I am concerned about you and your career. The team doctor, Venezuela and I all agree that you are healthy. There is nothing more we need to do for you.

You are healed and fully capable of returning to work. I won't continue to take your money. I'm releasing you."

I waited a beat before adding. "I can refer you to a psychotherapist when you're ready to admit you are hesitant to return to playing ball. No one will have to know. It will be between the two of us and the therapist."

DeMarco didn't say a word. He stared back at me, speechless.

I stood, deciding not to push him any further. "Let's eat. Dinner is ready."

Something like relief appeared in his eyes. "Good. I'm starving."

I turned toward the kitchen. It was time for him to end his pity party and get back to doing what he did best, playing football. I had to find a way to convince him, so I decided to call Rolonda later that evening after he left.

"Spring, you know DeMarco is sweet on you, right?"

I sighed. "I don't know. At first, I thought he was just flirting, but in Vegas, he seemed serious."

"Oh yes, I remember seeing the two of you locking lips when we came back from dinner on his friend's yacht. Well..."

"Well, what?" I snapped. I'd called her to get her help about her cousin's lack of interest to return to the field. My love life wasn't the issue here.

Rolonda sighed. "Girl, are you interested in DeMarco or not?"

"I'm considering it. We talk all the time, we go out all the time now. I don't want to rush into anything. You know what happens when you rush. Fools rush in. Plus, he is related to you, so I want to make sure this will work. And, he's an athlete. Ro, you know my history. Why are you pushing?"

Rolonda was silent for a moment. "I feel you and I know you've been hurt in the past. But, sis, DeMarco is a great catch. I don't want you to break his heart."

"Well, since you're so concerned about DeMarco, what do you think about him returning to the football field?"

"What do you mean? I'm sure once he is healed and released to return to playing ball, he will."

I had released him.

Obviously, Rolonda did not know he was well enough to play. Knowing how DeMarco reacted when I suggested he talk to a therapist, it probably wasn't a good idea to bring his reluctance up to a family member.

Rolonda interrupted my thoughts. "Sis, all I'm saying is you better hurry up and get that man before someone with a big butt and a big smile comes along and scoops him up."

"If we're meant to be, he will wait for me to decide what's best for me. I'm not trying to break his heart. I'm trying to protect mine. I know he is used to ladies running and jumping all over him, but I am not the one. Besides, I have a big butt and a big smile."

Rolonda laughed. "Yes, girl. Yes, you do."

I chuckled. "Later, soror."

"Good night, sis."

After ending the call with Rolonda, I sat on the couch thinking. I hoped Rolonda and I didn't end up falling out. It could be a good thing to date someone related to a close friend or it could be a bad thing. It was important that Rolonda mind her business regarding DeMarco and me.

I knew I had to decide, but I could do without the pressure.

Chapter Nine

DeMarco and I started dating regularly. On today's date, he introduced me to mini-golf, which I was surprised how much I liked. He stood close behind me while giving instructions. His strong hand guided me while showing me how to hit the ball. Mesmerized by the closeness of his body pressed against mine, when DeMarco asked me if I understood his instructions, I mumbled, "Uh huh."

"Girl, you are actually pretty good at this," DeMarco chuckled. "Look at you enjoying yourself. It's good to see you relaxed and open to trying new things."

I was blushing like a coy, little girl. "I am enjoying mini-golf. Thanks for bringing me, DeMarco."

He stared at me, his eyes sincere. "You need to give me a chance, Spring."

My heart fluttered. I eyed him back. "I'm trying."

I didn't miss the glimmer of hope in DeMarco's eye before he turned back to swing the golf club.

He is a chocolate delight and I do have a sweet tooth. I have to trust someone someday.

We walked hand in hand back to DeMarco's car after playing a few more rounds of mini-golf.

"Baby, every Sunday after church, my parents host a family dinner and I would like for you to go with me tomorrow to meet my family."

My hand shook. I tightened my grip on DeMarco's hand so he couldn't feel me trembling. "That would be nice, DeMarco. Maybe some other time."

He frowned. "Spring, I'm not going to take no for an answer. I already told them you were coming." He pointed his finger at me. "I'll pick you up for church, and then we're going to my parent's house for dinner and that's that."

I stomped my feet like a two-year-old. "You can't tell me what to do, DeMarco!"

He grinned. "I can and I will. And, you better be ready when I pick you up in the morning, woman!" He leaned in to hug me. "My parents already love you, Spring. You have nothing to worry about."

I answered with a smile, "Okay, sir." This would be the first time I've seen his parents since I visited him in the hospital after he was injured. I'm sure between Rolonda and DeMarco, his parents had heard plenty about our growing relationship.

Both in our own thoughts, we were quiet on the short ride from the golf course to my house.

DeMarco walked me to my door. "I am going home to shower. I'm worn out." He leaned in and gave me a juicy kiss. "See you tomorrow."

After he left, I leaned against the door. "That man has some sexy lips," I chuckled.

After church, DeMarco drove us to his family home. Once inside, he grinned at the mature couple who stood in the foyer. "Mom and Dad, this is Spring. Spring, meet my parents."

I held out my hand. "Nice to meet you, Mr. and Mrs. Blues."

DeMarco's mom hugged me instead, and then stepped back. "Nice to meet you, Spring. We have heard so many good things about you. Please make yourself comfortable. I must go back in the kitchen." She turned to leave and then looked back at me. "Next time you come, you will be in the kitchen helping me."

"Yes, ma'am," I nodded. "I sure will."

The delicious aroma of the food drifted into the foyer of the grand house. There was enough food on the table to feed an army. Mrs. Blues had prepared a huge turkey and dressing, asparagus, string beans, potato salad, homemade rolls that were to die for, pecan pie and chocolate cake.

I was glad I had worn a skirt with an elastic waistband. Throughout dinner, DeMarco's mom kept throwing out hints of marriage. *I guess she liked me.*

Once again, I was getting cold feet. I felt like I needed to back away and stop making myself so available. I was struggling with giving my heart to DeMarco, and certainly was not ready for his family to accept me so willingly.

Maybe I was worrying unnecessarily. Maybe I needed to spend some time alone. I would let DeMarco know that next weekend was all mine. I could make it a Netflix and chill weekend. Do some soul searching and thinking for a few days.

After DeMarco dropped me off, the loneliness of my home quickly engulfed me. I undressed and began to cry like a fool. I mean, one of those ugly cries where my eyes were swollen, and I was a snotty, sobbing hot mess. I went into the bathroom and looked at myself in the mirror.

I chided myself. "Now is all of this necessary? Look at you. Clarence has gone on with his life and here you are whimpering like a weak fool, talking about 'I, Spring Vaughn, do not date athletes.' But you're the first person at church on Sunday morning talking about being positive, be strong, be wise and look at you! Stop this madness right now, Spring."

A still small voice whispered.

I sent him.

"Huh?"

I sent him. I removed the last man and I sent him.

I looked around the room and saw no one.

My eyes returned to the mirror. I knew it was the voice of the Great I Am. I wiped my eyes.

I knew what I needed to do.

Chapter Ten

Despite my moment of clarity on Sunday evening, I had purposely kept my distance from DeMarco most of the week. Doubts still lingered. The phone rang three times before I looked at the caller ID. *Can't avoid him forever, it's been three days.* "Hello?"

"Spring, is that you?"

I rolled my eyes. "DeMarco, who else is it going to be? Were you calling one of your other women and accidentally dialed my number?"

"No, no. Look, no. I told you I was a one woman at a time man. It's just...Well, I've been calling and calling. I'm...I'm a little shocked you answered."

"I thought it might be important." I hesitated. "Are you okay? You didn't hurt yourself again, did you? Your ankle is okay?"

"My ankle is fine, Spring." DeMarco blew out a breath. "Look, ummm, do you think you could come over? I know it's late, but I have some things I need to say and I'd rather talk to you in person."

"Okay. Yea, sure. I'll come over. Give me an hour, I need to freshen up and change."

"Okay, I'll be here." DeMarco hung up the phone before I could say anything more.

"That was weird. I wonder what he wants." I headed toward my bathroom. "He sounded
strange. He said his ankle was fine, but he hung up so abruptly."

I shook my head. "Let me get my behind in the shower. I am no longer going to let what happened in the past stop me from living a fulfilled life."

I showered and dressed in a sexy dress that showed all my curves, and then spritzed myself with my favorite fragrance before adding a few touches of makeup to my lips and brows. I slipped my feet into a pair of sexy ankle strap heels and headed out to my car.

Sixty minutes later, I sat in front of DeMarco's home and took a deep breath to gather myself before I got out of the car. I pressed the intercom button on the panel and knocked on the door. "DeMarco, it's me. Spring."

"Doors unlocked for you. Come on in." DeMarco's voice replied through the speaker.

I opened the door and laid my bag on the table in the foyer. "DeMarco?" I called out, walking down the hall. I could hear music from the speakers he had throughout his home. I reached the dining room and stopped. There were candles lit and a spread of food on the table with two place settings.

DeMarco appeared with a kitchen towel thrown over his shoulder. His eyes raked over her body. "You look beautiful, Spring."

My knees went weak at the sound of my name, smooth as silk, on his tongue.

He approached me, reaching for my hand. I wondered if he could see the fear in my eyes.

Barely able to find my voice, I whispered. "What's all this?"

DeMarco pulled me close to him and kissed me gently on the lips.

"I missed you," he whispered against my quivering lips. His hands caressed my back like a feather causing a chill to run down my body. Inside, I was a nervous wreck. He led me by the hand to the table and used his free hand to pull a chair out, beckoning me to take the seat. He filled our glasses with sweet red wine and then took the seat beside me.

I grabbed my glass and drank the contents all at once.

"Slow down, lush." DeMarco laughed and refilled my glass.

This loosened me up. I relaxed, choosing to surrender to whatever was next for me and DeMarco. The man was handsome, kind, understanding, and a one-woman man. I had heard from the Great I Am that I had found my man. I was going to stop denying my feelings and give him a chance.

I looked at the food on the table — lamb chops, red potatoes, asparagus, salad, homemade rolls and a hot apple pie. "You made this delicious meal?"

He chuckled. "No, I can't cook. The cook made it before she left for the evening."

"It looks delicious, and I'm hungry. Let's dive in."

DeMarco grinned from ear to ear.

We finished dessert, and DeMarco relaxed while I cleared the table and loaded the dishes in the dishwasher as if I was the lady of the house. I could tell from his wide grin that he loved it. With the table cleared and the kitchen in order, we refilled our wine glasses and went into the living room. Flames glowed from the wood crackling in the fireplace, providing ambiance.

I curled up on the couch next to DeMarco. He massaged my back while we watched television. His big strong hands felt good caressing my body. He bent and placed sweet kisses on my neck.

"You smell so good, Spring."

I peered up at him. "You smell pretty good yourself."

He kissed me on my neck again. I was fascinated by how a big man like DeMarco could be so gentle. I felt a tingle and a jolt shoot through my body. I did not want him to stop. I was losing control which was not what I wanted to do. I shook my head to clear it.

He stood, took my hand and led me to his bedroom. I was glad he helped me to the room because my knees were weak, and I was afraid they would give out.

Like something out of a fairytale, a large poster bed adorned the center of his huge bedroom. DeMarco picked me up like the gentle giant he was and laid me in the middle of the bed on top of the comforter.

"DeMarco, I want to spend the night with you, but I need to remind you that I'm not engaging in intercourse. I have vowed to remain celibate until marriage. If that's a problem, I need to know now before we get too carried away."

"I respect that, Spring. If you gave it up that easily, you would be like all the other women I have met in my life."

"Really?"

"Really, darling. A virtuous woman is just what I am looking for in a wife."

"Wife?"

"You heard me. I said wife."

I murmured. "Hmmm, Spring Blues. That has a nice ring to it."

DeMarco and I fell asleep in each other's arms. I woke up in the middle of the night and got out of bed searching for my shoes and purse.

"Spring. Girl, where do you think you are going in the middle of the night? Get back in bed and go to sleep." DeMarco sat up, his voice was heavy with sleep.

I laughed and tugged on his shirt before crawling back into bed, relieved to have someone to snuggle with for a change. DeMarco was a sweet man. We snuggled in a spoon position before falling back to sleep, comfortable and content.

When I woke again, it was morning. The tweeting birds coupled with the bright
sunshine pouring into the room through the open curtains lulled me from my peaceful sleep.

I sat up and stretched my arms, smiling. I couldn't remember the last time I had slept that well. I looked around the room, wondering where DeMarco was. The aroma of food wafted in from the kitchen. I quickly showered in the en-suite bathroom and crawled back into the California king bed. The door opened, and Demarco entered with a breakfast tray and coffee.

"Dang, girl, you sure can snore."

I burst out laughing. "I see you have jokes this morning."

I grabbed DeMarco's hand and said a prayer over our food and relationship.

"Did the cook come early and fix this too? Or is this all you?" I asked after biting into a buttery pastry.

DeMarco grinned and joined me in the bed. Shoulders touching as we shared a morning meal, I was content. It had been a long time since I allowed myself to be swept away and cared for.

We finished eating and DeMarco sat the tray on the nightstand. He turned on the huge flat screen TV. "Let's watch the football game."

"Okay, but you'll have to explain the game to me. I know nothing about football except there are a bunch of men in tight clothes, big shoulder pads and helmets knocking one another down."

"Don't worry," DeMarco thread his fingers through hers. "I'll teach you. I'll be returning back to the field and you need to know what you are watching, my dear."

I beamed. "That is great news, DeMarco!"

I rested my head on his shoulder, listening as DeMarco explained what was going on in the game. I never imagined being interested in football, but once I got the hang of the game, I began to enjoy it. The game was not as complicated as I thought it would be. I noticed how DeMarco came to life while talking about football. He was passionate about the sport. I looked forward to going to a live game and watching him play.

He turned to look at me. His eyes made me think he could be equally passionate about me. I had a glimpse of my future and the many opportunities I would enjoy with this man and him on the field in this game.

I guess the old saying is true, there is someone for everyone and love is stronger than hate. I, Spring Vaughn, was dating an athlete. Love had called my name.

About the Author

Annie M. Johnson has enjoyed reading since a very early age. She remembered joking and saying often after reading books, "I can do that, I can write a book." Her first book, *Favor* was published in 2005. Since then, she has written and published *Holiday Mayhem, Survivor Seduction Aboard the SS Sunshine*, and *Life's Song a Miracle*. *Torn* was published with Peace in The Storm Publishing. *Powerful Woman Where Does Your Power Come From?* was published with Imani Faith Publishing.

The Replacement Date
Tyora Moody

1

For the third time in the past hour, I smiled at myself in the mirror trying to convince myself this would be the perfect evening.

You can do this, Donna Madison. It's only been fifteen years since you've been out on a date. It's like riding a bike.

My smile faltered. I never liked dating. In fact, I never even learned how to properly ride a bike.

I sighed deeply as I smoothed my dress down across my stomach. I hated my belly. Tonight, I would have to trust the control-top brief to keep the pooch in place. My body represented a woman in her mid-forties who despised exercise and relished her snacks a bit too much.

The dress was new for this occasion, since nothing in my closet served the purpose. I'm usually a neutral girl, but I couldn't resist the coral dress when I passed by it in *Belk*. It was fitted at the waist and swung around my short legs as I walked. I turned to the side to peer down at my shoes. I'm not one for heels, but the bronze low-heel sandals added a sophistication that I needed. Not to include some height. They were surprisingly comfortable too. Even my natural hair was not working against me tonight. I had it twisted all week and decided to remove the twists, so my hair hung around my shoulders.

I placed my hands on my ample hips. "Not bad. Not bad at all."

It's been a long time since I spent this much time on myself. Now, if only I could get through tonight.

It was a breezy Friday night in May when I walked out of my house towards my KIA Optima. Friday nights were usually spent curled up reading a book or binge-watching Netflix. I cringed, smelling rain approaching in the atmosphere.

Rain, rain, stay away.

To head off any pending disasters, I checked the back seat of my car to make sure my handy umbrella was on the floor. I believed in being prepared. But despite all my preparation, my stomach twisted with nerves I forgot existed. I couldn't believe I was actually going on a date.

I started the engine and backed out the driveway of the two-story home I used to share with my ex-husband. The house was awarded to me during the divorce settlement. I was grateful since I'd spent so much time making the house a home. I had hoped to move on with my life.

Except I hadn't.

I turned forty-five last month. And in the last five years, I'd given up on love, choosing not to date. I loved with my whole heart once and the heartbreak had been too much. Ten years of my life was blown to bits in one day when Allen Reynolds handed me divorce papers.

Okay, maybe I exaggerate about the explosion part. If I was honest with myself, which I tend to not be sometimes, ten years had started out fabulously then slowly grew cold and, five years later, were now a distant memory.

Really, by the end of the marriage, I barely recognized the man I'd married.

I blew out a breath as I drove. I wasn't bitter. Okay, not anymore. But sometimes mulling over the past did something to me emotionally. Failure was hard to swallow, especially for something I desired so badly.

What little girl doesn't want her Prince Charming to sweep her off her feet into a life of happily ever after? What can you do as your dream slowly slips away?

My Prince Charming was a breath of fresh air. I was thirty years old and already avoiding dating when he dropped into my life. We met at church, and I just knew God sent him my way.

I was helping my mom and aunt Judy in Victory Gospel's church kitchen. Allen's family was using the church fellowship hall for their family reunion dinner. My mom and her sister, known for their catering business for years, were obvious choices. I didn't take after my mom in the cooking department, but I did alright and helped out when I could.

That day, I was the designated person to scoop potato salad on plates. I almost dropped the plate when my eyes locked with a chocolate man with a bright white smile staring back at me. Later, while I was helping with the clean-up, Allen approached me. The following week, we met for dinner. We dated for nine months before he proposed.

My mama and everyone around me kept commenting about how fast we were moving. Mama thought I was pregnant. Not!

What I didn't see coming was being replaced ten years later. The replacement wife was a decade younger than me with the kind of body I could never have if I tried.

She also delivered on something I never could. A son.

A child was never to come from my body thanks to my enemy, endometriosis.

Allen always said not having children of his own didn't matter to him. I never figured out if the pregnancy with his mistress was accidental or not, but it didn't matter now since the child was being raised by Allen and his new wife. After I saw a photo of the happy couple on my timeline, I stayed away from Facebook for weeks. When I returned to social media, I unfriended and blocked any friends associated with Allen.

All that was in the past, and tonight it felt good to be out.

It wasn't like I was afraid of being alone. At least, I thought I wasn't. But lately, the sense that maybe it was time for a change had been stirring in my spirit.

I sighed deeply as I flowed with the busy traffic. Rush hour in Charlotte had slowed, but I-77 was still heavy with cars. I took the exit to I-85, headed towards Concord. This was a longer drive than I wanted, but I was determined not to have my date pick me up at my house. I wasn't quite ready for that.

The one person in the world who knew how much I didn't like matchmaking decided to do just that. Thank goodness, I trusted my long-time friend, Fatima Lawrence. Friends since third-grade, Fatima has known me for over thirty-seven years. When I didn't want to admit what was happening with my marriage, she recognized my deep sadness and prayed with me up until the divorce papers were signed.

Fatima had married her high school sweetheart. The two of them had been on and off more years than I could count, but they still were together. If anyone knew about marriage and its struggles, it was Fatima. A week ago, she told me, "God has someone for you."

I wasn't really banking on it being George Saunders.

Fatima had worked with George for years. She said he had a sense of humor and was not boring, despite his being an accountant.

We will see!

I steadied my thoughts as I drove to my destination, focusing instead on the oldies playing on the radio.

I pulled into the Carrabba's Italian Grill parking lot and cut off the engine. This is where things got tricky. My stomach had calmed down the last few minutes of my drive, but as soon as I turned the key in the ignition, the butterflies returned in full force. I was ten minutes early so I sat for a few minutes. Tonight's date was either going to be the change I needed or would have me scrambling back to the safety of my quiet non-social life.

Lord, I'm trusting you to help me out here.

I stepped out of the car and glanced at the sky. The sky remained clear, but I could still see clouds in the distance. I reached for the umbrella and tucked it under my arm before peeking at my phone.

I was still about five minutes early for the seven o'clock dinner date, and I was definitely hungry. I hadn't eaten anything since lunch. I hoped my hunger and nerves would settle down so I could enjoy my meal.

I swung the doors open and entered the restaurant. There was quite a crowd so I stood to the side seeking out signs of George. I had never met George in person, but Fatima supplied me with plenty of pictures. And last night, I friended him on Facebook, so this wasn't totally a blind date. There was some advantages to social media.

The crowd seemed to keep packing inside the doorway, so I inched my way to the hostess and asked, "Has George Saunders arrived?"

The hostess checked her list. "I don't have a Saunders. Can I take your name?"

I was a little perplexed. It was officially seven o'clock, and someone needed to get the table. I placed my name on the list, and then sat on the edge of a bench occupied by a group of college-aged women. As they chattered, I pulled out my phone to see if George had sent a text message.

There was nothing. I didn't like being late and frowned upon others' tardiness as well, especially on occasions like this. Despite the crowd, the hostess called out, "Madison."

Still a little worried, I popped up from the bench and followed her to a table in the back.

A few seconds later, a clean-cut, young man appeared and smiled down at me. "Ma'am, can I get you a drink?" He placed menus on the table.

"Sure, I'll start with a glass of water for now."

"Great. Will someone be joining you?"

My nerves wrapped around my heart a brief moment.

What if George didn't show?

I pushed the thought away. "Yes, my date will be arriving soon."

After the waiter left, I noted that my phone displayed ten minutes after seven. I tried to not let my nerves take over, but a full fifteen minutes had passed.

The waiter came back with my water. "Would you like to order an appetizer?"

I was really tempted, but I shook my head. "No, I'll wait."

I peered at my phone again and grimaced. It was Friday night and Charlotte's traffic remained heavy in some areas. I gripped the glass of water and took a sip. I often ate by myself, so I did what I usually did and kept busy with my phone. It occurred to me that most of my communication with George had been through Facebook Messenger. I wondered if he had sent a message and I missed it. I clicked to open the app, but none of the messages I saw were from George. By the time I responded to all the messages, another seven minutes had flown by.

The disappointment of George not showing started to weigh on me. Not to mention the fact that I was really hungry.

Should I just order something?

I searched the restaurant for my waiter.

I decided if George didn't show in the next five minutes, I wasn't going to waste my entire evening. And I would most certainly call Fatima and tell her what I thought about her matchmaking skills.

I passed the time looking through my emails. Most of them, I usually ignored and should have unsubscribed from a long time ago.

A shadow crossed over my face, and I felt the presence of a tall figure standing by the table before I looked up. I peered up with expectancy, hoping my eyes wouldn't flash the anger I was feeling from waiting so long.

My eyes locked on the hovering figure. For a brief moment, it felt like everyone else in the restaurant faded into the background.

The man who stood in front of me was definitely not George.

My eyes stretched in surprise, and after I stopped blinking in disbelief, a smile spread across my face. This man was even better than George. A gorgeous man of maturity with a hint of gray around his temples, his eyes were just as brown and bright as they had been when he was much younger.

Some part of my brain told me my mouth was wide open and I snapped it shut. "Maxwell?" I stuttered. I hadn't spoken that name in years.

Maxwell Anderson grinned at me. "Yep. Donna Madison. It's good to see you." He stepped back. "Wait, didn't you get married?"

I shooed the question away like a fly had appeared in front of me. "I was married for a while, but I've been divorced for five years now. I went back to my maiden name."

Some of my excitement at seeing him deflated as I remembered. "How's your wife and family?"

Something like sadness shifted over his face, and his smile slipped away. "I'm widowed now, I'm afraid. Just me and the kids."

"Oh no. I'm so sorry to hear that. That must be hard."

"Being a single dad has definitely been a transition. How long has it been since we've seen each other?"

I sighed. So much regret was in that sigh, but I couldn't help it. I had crushed hard on this man for years. "At least fifteen years."

He looked around before directing his hand to the seat across from me. "Is someone joining you? I don't want to interrupt."

George had clearly been forgotten. I glanced down at my phone. It was already seven forty-five. "You can have a seat. I was supposed to meet someone at seven o'clock, but I think they may have stood me up."

The smile returned to Maxwell's face as he pulled out the chair in front of me.

I was mesmerized by his face. Maxwell lived down the street from me most of my life so we'd walk home from school together all the way up to graduation. I remembered a time when I dreamed that he and I would marry. Perhaps he was shocked to see me after all this time, but I don't think I was the only one mesmerized. Maxwell's eyes were riveted on me as well.

"I'm really sorry about your wife. How long has it been, if you don't mind me asking?"

I looked down at the table, scolding myself for the intrusion. Clean hands, fingernails clipped, and he still wore his wedding ring. *He must have really loved her.*

"It's been about two years now. Breast cancer."

My heart fell. I knew that must have been hard. "I'm so sorry. If I remember, you had three children together?"

His face beamed with pride. "Twin boys and a girl."

A pang of regret hit me. I always had that sense of loss when others talked about children. That was something I would never get to say.

Maxwell must have noticed something in my face. "What about you?"

"I couldn't have kids."

He reached across and squeezed my hand. "I'm so sorry, Donna. I remember you were really good with kids at vacation bible school."

I grinned. "I still am. VBS is back next month. I'm a Sunday School teacher too."

"Still at Victory Gospel Church? I'm planning to attend on Sunday."

That warmed my heart. "Yes, Victory Gospel is still home." I frowned. "How long have you been back in Charlotte?" *And how did I not know he was back?*

"We moved here a few months ago from Atlanta. I got a promotion to Reliance Financial's Southeast region headquarters which happens to be in Charlotte. My kids weren't happy about the move taking them from their friends, but it's good to be back home. I've caught up with so many friends I hadn't talked to in years. I was hoping I'd run into you."

Out the corner of my eye, I saw the waiter approach.

"I see your guest finally arrived," the waiter smiled. "Are you ready to order?"

I looked at Maxwell instead of correcting the waiter. "You hungry?"

He flipped open the menu. "Sure, let's eat."

After we placed our order, a comfortable silence settled between us. I wondered if Maxwell was soaking in this time as much as I was. I noticed he kept turning his ring around on his finger.

He finally broke the silence. "You said fifteen years ago was the last time we saw each other in person?"

I leaned forward. "Yes, I remember it was a few months before my wedding."

He cocked his head. "Oh."

"And..." I hesitated as the occasion dawned on me. I wasn't sure if I should bring it up. "It was your mom's funeral."

I watched him wince. That time in his life seemed to hit him all over again. His mother had lost a battle with cancer too. I couldn't imagine the depth of his pain at losing his wife to the same battle.

He nodded. "You're right. I remember now. That was a tough time for me. Alison had just had the twins a year before Mom received her diagnosis. She was pregnant with Ashlee. Mom never met her granddaughter."

I nodded, swallowing the lump in my throat. I remembered Maxwell's mom well. She was my mom's best friend. "Ashlee. That's a pretty name. What are the boy's names?"

He grinned. "Alex and Adrian. They're twins, but just as opposite as they can be. Alex is the athlete, more like me. Adrian is quiet and studious like his mother."

"So, they are all teenagers now? That must be rough."

He nodded. "They're good kids. They all have matured beyond their years losing their momma. They look out for me sometimes even better than I look out for them."

The waiter returned with our food. Even though I was beyond hungry, I took time to savor my lasagna. I wasn't sure what to think of how my evening turned out, but I didn't want to rush through it. I was grateful Maxwell was my date tonight.

A replacement date, Donna.

Maybe God felt like we both needed each other tonight.

The conversation continued long after our plates were cleared. We even opted for dessert.

I scooped up the last of my strawberry cheesecake as Maxwell asked, "So, what happened to your date? Is this someone you're serious about?"

I'm glad I waited to take the last bite because I probably would have choked. I snorted. "No, this was my first date in years." My cheeks grew warm.

Did I really just blurt that out to him?

His fork lingered over his tiramisu as his eyebrows shot up. "Really?"

I grimaced. "Remember Fatima? She set me up on this date tonight."

He starting laughing. "I remember Fatima. She liked doing that sort of thing." He placed his elbows on the table. "I hope you tell her she needs to get out of the matchmaking business."

"Oh believe me, I will."

He fiddled with his fork before placing it on the dessert plate. "It was good to run into you tonight. You're still beautiful, Donna."

Did someone just turn the heat up in the restaurant?

My face was already on fire, and now the heat was creeping down my shoulders and my back. I clutched my hands under the table and mumbled a thank you. This man and I had spent a lot of time together growing up, and I couldn't recall Maxwell ever complimenting me like that in the past. We were best friends. Him seeing me as beautiful didn't seem possible.

I looked down at our empty dessert plates and realized this evening had to come to an end. I turned my attention back to him. His eyes were still riveted on me. I remembered getting lost in the intensity of those eyes when I was younger. I wasn't that young girl anymore, but I still felt the same. I cleared my throat in an attempt to control my whirring emotions and looked around.

"Were you meeting someone here? We've talked all night, and I never asked why you were here."

He shook his head. "No, I was actually on my way home from work. I have a friend who's a manager here. He's supposed to cater an event at my job in a few weeks, and I thought I would check in. But..." Maxwell held his head down as if in shame. "I actually never... never... Well, I saw you. You were sitting alone and I just walked over." He smiled, stretching his hands out in front of him. "And, here I am."

I didn't know how to respond, so we sat there grinning at each other for what should have been a really awkward moment. Knowing what I remembered about Maxwell, he didn't believe in coincidences either.

Maxwell leaned in. "I'd like to meet with you again."

I didn't think it was possible to grin any bigger than I was already grinning. But, with the way the evening had gone, it didn't hurt to ask. "Are you asking me out for a real date?"

He flashed a smile. "Technically, we had a date tonight."

I rolled my eyes. "Yeah, more like a replacement date."

"So, let's do this for real next time. How about I pick you up from your house next Friday? We can go out for dinner and a movie? A real date where you won't get stood up."

I squeezed my hands together under the table. "Sure, I would enjoy catching up with you."

We exchanged phone numbers and stepped out the restaurant. It was the first time I'd noticed the rain. Even though we sat near a window, my focus never wavered from Maxwell. I opened my umbrella.

"Let me hold that for you." Maxwell extended his hand.

More conscious of his spicy cologne than I was when we were inside, I passed the umbrella handle to him. His shoulder touched mine as he held the umbrella high above both of us. Caught up in Maxwell's closeness, I barely remembered walking to my car.

"I'll call you," he commented after I opened my car door.

"Great, I look forward to talking to you."

With a wink, Maxwell trotted away to a dark SUV that wasn't very far from my car.

I sat inside my car for a few minutes, trying to grasp what actually happened over the last few hours. I had a feeling my sleep tonight would be full of sweet dreams for the first time in a really long time.

2

The next morning, Fatima and Kim sat in my kitchen staring at me as I relayed the events from last night.

Kim exclaimed, "What happened to George? How did you just get a blast from the past as your date?"

I looked over at Kim before answering. With the way she was side eyeing me, if I didn't know her any better, I would've thought she was jealous. But, I've known Kim Wilson since college. Previously married for a few years herself, Kim now opted for perpetual dating. I couldn't imagine introducing myself to strange men over and over again. But she did and had the stories to tell. I got a kick out of her dating horror stories, but deep down I think Kim just didn't like to be alone.

I explained. "According to the message I received about ten o'clock last night, George had to rush to the hospital for an emergency. Apparently. his youngest son fell and ended up breaking his arm."

Fatima held her head in her hands. "He still should have called you. I'm sorry he just stood you up."

I shook my head. "It was his child. If it was one of you and your children were hurt, they would be priority too."

Fatima shook her head. "George still carries a torch for his ex-wife too."

Kim yelped before I could. "What? You knew this and you still set him up with Donna?"

"Really?" I giggled and shrugged my shoulders. "I'm fine, Kim. But to answer your other question, it was a chance meeting running into Maxwell. Not a big deal."

Fatima peered at me. "Umm, no. It is a big deal." She wiggled her eyebrow. "God is obviously the better matchmaker here."

Though I secretly agreed, I wasn't going to admit that to Fatima or Kim. I reached for my empty coffee mug and then grabbed the carafe. "Last night was me having dinner with an old friend. That's it. Besides, he still hasn't gotten over his wife. He said it's been two years since her death, but he was still wearing his wedding ring."

Kim shook her head. "Yeah, but he was interested in seeing you again, right?"

I almost spilt the coffee and concentrated on holding my shaking hand steady while I poured. "He mentioned he had been wanting to connect with old friends."

Fatima placed her cup in the kitchen sink. "Old friends. You two were best friends. So, when do you plan to meet again?"

"Friday." I rubbed my nose. "He has three teenagers though. I'm sure he's a very busy single dad. He might change his mind."

Fatima placed her arm around me. "Not a chance. His kids are going to love you."

I arched my eyebrow at my friend. "Let's not go that far yet."

I'd already spent too much time thinking about Maxwell as a single dad. Could it really work to have a relationship with him? Would his kids even accept another woman in his life?

Fatima kept going as if I hadn't said anything. "This is your chance. You and Maxwell were like this when you were younger." She crossed her fingers together and held them in front of me. "I never understood how the two of you just remained friends. You were crazy about him and he loved him some Donna."

"You mean you guys never dated?" Kim blurted.

I shook my head. "No, we were just best friends. He lived down the street from me. We've known each other since we were like nine years old."

"Wow!" Kim's incredulous look turned contemplative. "I never understood how a man and woman could just be friends. Seems impossible especially the older you get."

Fatima sighed as if expressing a point for the hundredth time. "A relationship should start with friendship. It should be the foundation of any relationship. You should be able to be yourself and unconditionally accept the other person in your life, flaws and all."

"Whatever." Kim scraped the rest of her yogurt cup. "I will say something is different about you this morning, Donna. You're glowing!"

"I am not." I protested. I don't know why I was trying to deny Fatima and Kim the satisfaction of seeing me happy. I guess deep down I didn't want to be disappointed. I had loved this man for a good portion of my young life. As a teenager, I stood on the sidelines, watching my friend grow into a handsome athlete, attracting the attention of what felt like most of the girls at our school. And then he went off to college, came home less and less, and our friendship faded.

I never found another male like Maxwell. I was able to be myself with him, and I truly enjoyed being around him. My ex-husband Allen was clearly a fluke. His good looks fooled me for a little while, but I didn't have the friendship with him that I had with Maxwell. Maxwell and I spent so much time together. We had known each other so well, we finished each other's sentences.

The bond that had always been between us was there again last night. How else could we have fallen into that comfortable rhythm of being together after fifteen years? And, why would God bring us together when we were both single for the first time in a long time?

I hoped this was more than just a chance meeting with an old friend.

3

Maxwell kept his promise. He called Saturday night and I lost track of how long we talked. I just know when we finally got off the phone it was close to one o'clock in the morning. I did catch a glimpse of him with his kids at Victory Gospel on Sunday. His daughter was almost as tall as me from what I could tell, and the boys had their dad's height.

My heart longed to move in that direction, but logic kept my feet planted. I wanted to be in Maxwell's presence, but convinced myself to let him and his kids enjoy the day. Before I made it out the sanctuary, I felt someone touching my arm. When I turned, Maxwell stood so close, he practically took my breath away. Like Friday night, it was as if everyone around me disappeared.

How had he made it over to me so fast? Victory Gospel Church had a large membership trying to pile out the doors. "Maxwell, I see you found me."

He smiled. "I saw you when you came in so I knew which direction to head. I know you and I have a date Friday, but I was wondering if you would be interested in joining us for dinner next Sunday?"

"Us? You mean, you and your kids?"

He nodded. "We're living in my mom's house. I was still managing the upkeep while I was away."

I frowned. "You moved back into your childhood home? Really, how have we not ran into each other before now?"

"I know, right? I've been wondering about that too. The neighborhood and the school system is still good. Even better than when we were growing up there." He shrugged. "Just never been able to let go of the house. I've been renting it out for years. After Alison died, I decided to pour some money into renovating. It really doesn't look like the same house."

I looked around, stumbling a bit with my words. "Wow, I would love to see what you've done with the house. Next Sunday?"

"Just me and the kids. I wanted to introduce them. They are always interested in people I knew when I was younger."

Meet his kids.

Maxwell's eyes held a hint of concern. "Is that okay? It will be a simple meal."

I cocked my head. "You cook?"

That smile of his returned. "My daughter and I cook together. She's probably the better cook since she cooked all the time with her mom."

I nodded, still grasping the invitation. "Does she know you invited me?"

"Yes, my kids know I invited a guest. They're excited to meet you."

I smiled. "Okay."

He winked. "Looks like we will be seeing a lot of each other."

Instead of following Maxwell out, I stood and watched his retreating back. It took me a minute to realize I was clutching the back of the pew as if I needed support.

I was planning to stop by my mother's house this afternoon. If Maxwell had moved in right down the street, Mama should have known that.

Funny, she never mentioned it.

My mother still lived in the same house where I grew up, a few houses down from Maxwell's mother's house. I couldn't believe it was now *his* home.

I pulled out my key and entered my childhood home. The house was quiet and lacked the usual smells of Sunday cooking. I called out, "Mama, are you here yet?"

My mama yelled down. "I'm up here, Donna, changing out of my church clothes."

I headed up the stairs to catch my mom slipping into a sundress. I didn't blame her, summer was a month away, but the temperatures were in the high eighties today.

She smiled. "Hey, I didn't see you at church today."

I reached over to hug her. "I was there. I slipped into the sanctuary after cleaning up the Sunday School classroom. The class created a bit of a mess today."

"Well, I'm taking a break from cooking today. Beulah invited me over to her house. I'm sure she wouldn't mind if I brought another person. She always has plenty of food."

Beulah Samuels was one of mom's oldest friends. I was tempted to join them, but felt the need for some alone time this afternoon. "No, I just wanted to come and check on you."

Mama raised her eyebrow. "Check on me? Donna, everything okay?"

I sat down on the edge of Mama's bed. "Did you know Maxwell was back?"

Mama placed her hands on her hip. "I did. I thought you did too. I meant to ask you about it. I just kept forgetting. I noticed he has kids. They have to be teenagers. I haven't seen a woman though."

Figures. Nothing happened around here that Mama didn't know.

"His wife died a few years ago. Breast cancer."

Mama sat down on the bed beside me. "Oh my. That's awful. Same thing that took his mom out of this world. Bless his heart."

"We ran into each other on Friday. Had dinner and talked. He invited me to Sunday dinner next week."

Mama smiled. "Well, that can't be a bad thing. Who's cooking?"

I laughed. "Apparently he and his daughter are the cooks."

Mama nodded. "Sounds like you're going to have an interesting afternoon."

I cleared my throat. "And we're going out on a date. A real date on Friday."

Mama raised both eyebrows. "A real date?"

I told her about our unexpected date.

She sat for a few moments soaking in my story. "Well, that's something. The Lord does work in mysterious ways." She turned to me. "I'm glad you two are reacquainting. I remember how close you two were when you were younger. Sadie and I always used to wonder about you two."

I frowned. "Wonder what?"

Mama swatted my hands. "You know? If you two would get married. I remember how both of you fussed like an old couple when you were only what, nine years old. Sadie was kind of disappointed when Maxwell didn't ask you to the prom. He ended up asking that cheerleader."

My mind recalled that evening like it was yesterday. I too was hoping Maxwell would ask me. Instead, I attended my senior prom with a boy from my Sunday School class.

"Back then Maxwell saw me as one thing. His friend. Maybe that's the way he still sees me."

Mama placed her hand on my shoulder. "I'm sure Maxwell is remembering that one of the best people in his life was you. Sometimes it takes a while for people to appreciate us. We get off on the wrong paths, but God has a way of making those paths straight."

4

Like clockwork, around nine o'clock every night for a week, Maxwell and I talked on the phone, catching up on each other's lives. I almost felt like I knew his kids after our conversations. I knew how much Ashlee loved Instagram and Alex was following in his dad's footsteps on the basketball court. And, if I ever needed any computer help, Adrian was my boy.

Late Wednesday afternoon, while at my desk editing copy for a client's brochure, my cell phone rang. I looked at the caller ID.

"Hey, you," I answered with a smile. "Nice surprise."

Maxwell responded. "How's your day been?"

"Not bad. I'm wrapping up some edits for the day."

"You think you'll be ready to head home soon?"

I peered at the clock, four forty-five. Usually I stayed late to avoid sitting in traffic so I was looking at another hour. "Did you have something in mind?"

"I was hoping we could meet, maybe for coffee."

I couldn't keep the grin off my face if I tried. "Coffee sounds great. I know the perfect place. A lady from our church has a great place uptown right off College Street. It's called Southern Delights Cafe."

"Sounds like it's walking distance from my office."

"Mine too. I'll meet you there in thirty minutes?"

"That sounds great."

Despite our planned date only two days away, my skin tingled with giddiness over our impromptu coffee meeting. I had learned in one of our late night talks that Maxwell's office building was only a few streets over from mine. Like me, he parked in the nearby parking garages and battled with rush hour traffic. We've been so close to each other for months.

By the time I entered Southern Delights Cafe, Maxwell was already at a table with two cups of coffee.

"Wow, you already grabbed coffee."

"I remembered how much you liked caramel. Thought you might like the caramel latte." He dipped his head with a slight smile. "I hope I'm not being presumptuous."

I sat stunned. "You remembered that?"

"Oh yeah. You still eat Twix candy bars? Remember how you liked to eat the caramel off the cookie?"

I giggled. "I still do."

I'm not sure why I felt compelled to look, but I noticed Maxwell wasn't wearing his wedding ring. *When did he take it off?*

We chatted for an hour about the old days until Maxwell's phone rang. "Sorry, I need to take this. It's my daughter."

I nodded and sipped my remaining latte which had now grown cold. I watched Maxwell's face as he talked. His smile slipped away, replaced by a wrinkle in his eyebrow. His voice rose slightly. "Where are you? Alright calm down, I'll be there as soon as possible."

"Is everything okay?" I asked.

He shook his head. "Ashlee rode home with one of her friends and there was a car accident. I'm sorry, I need to go."

"Oh no, is Ashlee okay?"

"She said everything checked out at the hospital, but I wish someone had called me earlier."

"Where is she?"

"Carolinas Medical Center."

"Well, that's not far from here. You can get there in ten minutes, easy." I looked at his face. "Why don't you let me drive you? You look distraught."

He shook his head. "I couldn't ask you to do that."

I grabbed my keys. "I would feel better if you let me. My car is probably closer."

Maxwell looked like he wanted to protest again but followed me out. In ten minutes, we were on our way. I'm not sure what prompted me to interject myself into their family emergency, but helping Maxwell felt right.

We arrived at the hospital, and Maxwell inquired about his daughter. Someone led us to a room with the curtains closed, and Maxwell rushed to his daughter.

His daughter seemed smaller in person, but I'd only seen her from far away at church on Sunday. Her hair was braided and pulled up high in a ponytail. Ashlee had her dad's eyes which were now fixed on me.

"Dad, who's that?"

I cringed as Maxwell turned to face me. *Why did I do this again?* I should have stayed in the waiting room. It wasn't like I was family.

Maxwell's smile brought me some comfort.

"This is Donna Madison. She's coming to eat with us on Sunday, remember?"

Recognition entered her eyes. "Oh yeah, you and dad were best friends. I have a best friend who's a boy too."

Maxwell raised his eyebrow. "You do?"

"Yes, Ricky?" The tone of Ashlee's response implied her father should have already known this.

Still frowning, Maxwell patted his daughter's hand. "Okay. How are you doing? Where's the doctor?"

"I'm fine, Dad, ready to go home. Mrs. Lancaster's car is messed up in the back, but we didn't get a scratch on us."

Maxwell nodded. "As soon as I find the doctor, okay?" He turned to me. "Can you stay with her?"

I nodded. *Sure, I could stay with a girl I hardly knew.* But I've known her father most of my life. I stepped into the room and sat down in the chair. I knew, even at fourteen, she had to be shook up from the event.

"I'm so sorry this happened to you. You must have been scared."

She peered at me, her eyes taking me in head to toe. "I was at first, but when I realized I wasn't hurt, I was okay. I'm just worried about Mrs. Lancaster. She was pretty upset with the guy who ran into us."

"I can imagine. So, your dad says you're the cook?"

Ashlee smiled. "I learned a lot from my mom. I used to do a lot of baking with her. She also taught me how to cook rice, chicken and other stuff like that too. Dad's a pretty good cook too. He just works a lot sometimes."

"I see."

Ashlee found her phone and we ventured off into silence.

Maxwell showed up to break the awkwardness. "The doctor signed your discharge papers. We can get you home," he said to Ashlee.

As we headed out of the hospital towards my car, Maxwell turned to me. "You can drive me back to the garage and we can take it from there."

"Sure, not a problem," I nodded.

Once we were in the car, Maxwell placed his hands on my arm. "I really appreciate you being here with us today. You went out of your way."

Conscious of Maxwell's hand on my bare arm, I looked over at him. "That's what friends are for, Maxwell. Let me get you to your car." I peered over my shoulder. "I'm sure Ashlee is ready to get home."

I glanced in my rearview mirror as I drove and noticed Ashlee was watching me. I wasn't sure whether to be flattered or worried. She accepted that I was her dad's old friend from childhood. Would Maxwell's children accept a different type of relationship?

Once I entered the parking garage, Maxwell guided me to his SUV.

While Ashlee situated herself in their vehicle, Maxwell leaned towards my driver's door. I rolled my window down.

"Thank you, again. I'll see you on Friday."

I smiled. "I'm looking forward to it."

I floated on cloud nine the entire way home, elated that Maxwell was looking forward to our date on Friday. I was too.

It was Sunday afternoon with Maxwell's family that had me worried.

Were we doing too much too fast?

5

Friday night was all I expected and more. Growing up, Maxwell had been a huge Star Wars fan so it seemed fitting that we would watch *Solo*. He reminded me of a big kid.

After the movie, Maxwell dropped me off at my house and walked me to my porch. I turned to him. "I enjoyed my evening with you."

He cupped his hand under my chin. "I did as well."

Before I knew it, Maxwell's lips were on mine.

We were kissing. Maxwell and I were K-I-S-S-I-N-G.

He moved back, but not so far that I didn't feel the warmth of his body. "I'm really glad we connected again. I missed you."

I gulped, not expecting this proclamation. "I missed being around you too, Maxwell."

He winked. "Sleep tight, Donna. I'll see you on Sunday."

I smiled back. "I'm looking forward to the feast."

He laughed as he turned to head back to his SUV.

Once inside, I sprawled across my couch, and for the longest time, I held my fingers over my lips. Then I prayed. I prayed Maxwell and I were moving in a direction that wouldn't leave either one of us heartbroken.

Sunday arrived quickly and unlike Friday night, the pending occasion felt more like a test as I drove towards the Anderson home.

My thoughts plagued me all weekend. What if I failed to get along with his kids?

Maxwell greeted me warmly at the door with a hug. The first thing I noticed when I stepped into the living room was how different it appeared from when I came here as a child.

"You weren't kidding about the renovation. I mean it feels like the same house, but it looks totally different."

Maxwell's face beamed. "It does. I decided to knock down that wall so when you walk in you can see clear back to the kitchen."

I nodded. "I like it. The open concept works well."

"Make yourself at home. Ashlee is in the kitchen and the boys are upstairs. Dinner will be ready in about twenty minutes."

"Great." I watched as Maxwell joined his daughter in the kitchen. Whatever they were cooking smelled delicious.

I walked around the living room slowly, glancing at the photos on the shelf above the fireplace. My eyes fell on a photo frame of a woman I vaguely remembered meeting years ago.

Alison Anderson was very pregnant with Ashlee during Maxwell mother's funeral. When I walked over to give a condolences hug to Maxwell, his wife had glanced at me. He turned to introduce us.

"This was my dearest friend growing up."

That was how he introduced me to his wife. And, Alison had smiled at me like she'd known me all her life. I could tell then she was a remarkable woman. No wonder Maxwell couldn't give up his ring. He loved her. She was the mother of his children.

Suddenly, I wondered if I should be here in Maxwell's home.

I heard my name and turned around. Maxwell was standing with his two sons next to him. He smiled.

"These guys are probably a lot taller than you remember."

I cleared my throat, forcing back the emotions that were trying to overtake me. "The last time I saw these two, they were toddlers. Now, let me guess," I pointed to the young man wearing glasses, "you're Adrian." I swung around and pointed to the other boy. "Alex."

The boys nodded.

Maxwell beamed at me. "You ready to eat?"

"Yeah, did you need my help?" I offered.

"We got it." Maxwell pulled out a dining room chair. "You can grab a seat here."

I sat and watched as the Anderson family brought dishes to the table. Roasted chicken, green beans, macaroni and cheese and biscuits.

I was overwhelmed. "Wow, you guys went all out. Your momma would have been proud."

Maxwell grinned. "I agree. This was her kind of eating."

I was expecting us to eat in silence, but Maxwell bantered back and forth with his kids. I ate and watched, surprised that I felt comfortable joining in their conversation and laughter.

Despite protests, I helped clear the table and stacked the dishes in the dishwasher. By the time I shut the dishwasher, I turned to see that Maxwell and I were alone in the kitchen.

"I didn't scare the kids off, did I?"

He shook his head. "No, they all have their own worlds they wanted to get back to. I insist that we all eat together. It's the main time of day I can get a sense of what's going on in their world."

I nodded. "I noticed your no phones rule at the table."

"Actually, that's a rule Alison had. I used to be as bad as the kids, checking emails at the dinner table."

Silence fell on us. For a brief second, I felt like Alison was in the room with us. At least the memories of her were. Her family. Her rules.

Maxwell interrupted my thoughts. "Why don't we sit outside on the patio?"

"Sure."

I followed him outside, also not recognizing the patio. "You really did a lot of work out here. I remember when all of this was grass."

"I wanted a place for any of us to bring friends over and hang out." Maxwell looked pensive. "Are you okay? You seem quiet."

I wasn't sure how to respond, but then I remembered this was the man I grew up with and told everything. Well, mostly everything. I never really told him how I felt. "I'm good, this was good. I have to say I wasn't sure... I mean about meeting the kids. I'm assuming that it's good for them to meet an old friend."

Maxwell shook his head. "You are so much more than just an old friend. It was important to me for them to meet you. You were a big part of my life for so many years." He looked at me. "I never stopped thinking about you over the years."

Now was the time. Now or never. "Did you know how in love I was with you back then?"

Maxwell gawked at me. "What? No. I always thought you thought of me as a brother. I had the biggest crush on you growing up. I figured I wasn't smart enough for you or something."

I frowned. "Really? Well, I thought you didn't think I was one of the cool girls."

He laughed. "You were always the coolest. I could tell you anything and you wouldn't hesitate to set me straight."

I was in shock, not even sure what to say next. How come neither one of us realized the depth of our feelings back then?

Maxwell looked off into the yard, his eyes not really focusing. "Before she died, Alison told me to move on. That I needed to be happy." He turned to me. "I wasn't sure if I could move on. I had a great relationship with Alison, but I always had something special with you. I'm praying we can see where this goes."

He held out his hand.

For a minute, I forgot to breathe. Then I remembered what I'd been praying for and how I had sensed in my spirit it was time for a change.

"I can't wait to see what's next for us too."

I grasped his hand, filling the warmth of love that spread between us, awed and grateful by the sense of God's timing.

About the Author

Tyora Moody is the author of Soul-Searching Suspense books which include the *Reed Family Series*, *Eugeena Patterson Mysteries*, *Serena Manchester Series*, and the *Victory Gospel Series*. When Tyora isn't working for a client or doing something literary, she enjoys spending time with family, catching a movie on the big screen, and traveling. To contact Tyora about book club discussions or for book marketing workshops, visit her online at TyoraMoody.com.

www.ingramcontent.com/pod-product-compliance
Lightning Source LLC
Chambersburg PA
CBHW031607240626
47153CB00002B/662